Alfred Cookman

Familiar Hymns for Social Meetings

Alfred Cookman

Familiar Hymns for Social Meetings

ISBN/EAN: 9783337083724

Printed in Europe, USA, Canada, Australia, Japan

Cover: Foto ©Andreas Hilbeck / pixelio.de

More available books at **www.hansebooks.com**

☐ILIAR HYMNS

FOR

SOCIAL MEETINGS.

COMPILED BY

Rev. ALFRED COOKMAN.

New York:

PUBLISHED BY CARLTON & PORTER.

TRACT SOCIETY, 200 MULBERRY-STREET.

1864.

INTRODUCTORY NOTE.

THIS little volume has been arranged to meet the demand for a cheap pocket hymn book that might be used in the social services of the Church. The effort of the compiler has been to collate many of those old familiar hymns which by long and successful trial have earned for themselves a place in any book of song, and to associate with these some of the best of our popular choruses.

To make the collection available for army circulation we have incorporated a few patriotic songs.

May we not hope that this little hymn book will find a welcome in the homes and hearts of Methodists and other Christians everywhere?

CONTENTS.

PRAISE.

1
C. M.

Invitation to praise the Redeemer.

O FOR a thousand tongues, to sing
   My great Redeemer's praise;
The glories of my God and King,
   The triumphs of his grace.

2 My gracious Master, and my God,
   Assist me to proclaim,—
To spread, through all the earth abroad,
   The honors of thy name.

3 Jesus!—the name that charms our fears,
   That bids our sorrows cease;
'Tis music in the sinner's ears,
   'Tis life, and health, and peace.

4 He breaks the power of cancell'd sin,
   He sets the pris'ner free;
His blood can make the foulest clean;
   His blood avail'd for me.

2

Crown Him Lord of all.

ALL hail the power of Jesus' name
Let angels prostrate fall;
Bring forth the royal diadem,
And crown him Lord of all.

2 Sinners, whose love can ne'er forget
The wormwood and the gall;
Go, spread your trophies at his feet,
And crown him Lord of all.

3 Let every kindred, every tribe,
On this terrestrial ball,
To him all majesty ascribe,
And crown him Lord of all.

4 O that with yonder sacred throne
We at his feet may fall;
We'll join the everlasting song,
And crown him Lord of all.

3 L. M.

The Creation invited to praise God.

FROM all that dwell below the skies,
Let the Creator's praise arise;
Let the Redeemer's name be sung
Through every land, by every tongue.

2 Eternal are thy mercies, Lord;
Eternal truth attends thy word:
Thy praise shall sound from shore to shore,
Till suns shall rise and set no more.

3 Your lofty themes, ye mortals, bring;
In songs of praise divinely sing;
The great Salvation loud proclaim,
And shout for joy the Saviour's name.

4 In every land begin the song;
To every land the strains belong:
In cheerful sounds all voices raise,
And fill the world with loudest praise.

4   S. M.

Meeting, after absence.

AND are we yet alive,
   And see each other's face?
Glory and praise to Jesus give,
   For his redeeming grace.
Preserved by power divine
   To full salvation here,
Again in Jesus' praise we join,
   And in his sight appear.

2 What troubles have we seen!
   What conflicts have we pass'd!
Fightings without, and fears within,
   Since we assembled last!
But out of all the Lord
   Hath brought us by his love;
And still he doth his help afford,
   And hides our life above.

3 Then let us make our boast
   Of his redeeming power,
Which saves us to the uttermost,
   Till we can sin no more:
Let us take up the cross,
   Till we the crown obtain;
And gladly reckon all things loss,
   So we may Jesus gain.

5 L. M.

Tribute of praise to the Saviour.

JESUS, thou everlasting King,
  Accept the tribute which we bring;
Accept thy well-deserved renown,
And wear our praises as thy crown.

2 Let every act of worship be
Like our espousals, Lord, to thee:
Like the blest hour, when from above
We first received the pledge of love.

3 The gladness of that happy day,
O may it ever, ever stay:
Nor let our faith forsake its hold,
Nor hope decline, nor love grow cold.

4 Let every moment, as it flies,
Increase thy praise, improve our joys,
Till we are raised to sing thy name
At the great supper of the Lamb.

6 C. M.

Invitation to worship.

COME, let us join our cheerful songs
  With angels round the throne:
Ten thousand thousand are their tongues,
  But all their joys are one.

2 Worthy the Lamb that died, they cry,
  To be exalted thus:
Worthy the Lamb, our hearts reply,
  For he was slain for us.

3 Jesus is worthy to receive
  Honor and power divine;
And blessings more than we can give,
  Be, Lord, forever thine.

4 The whole creation join in one,
  To bless the sacred name
Of Him that sits upon the throne,
  And to adore the Lamb.

7   87, 87, 87, 87.

Hitherto hath the Lord helped us.

COME, thou Fount of every blessing,
  Tune my heart to sing thy grace;
Streams of mercy, never ceasing,
  Call for songs of loudest praise.
Teach me some melodious sonnet,
  Sung by flaming tongues above:
Praise the mount—I'm fix'd upon it;
  Mount of thy redeeming love!

2 Here I'll raise mine Ebenezer;
  Hither by thy help I'm come;
And I hope, by thy good pleasure, ·
  Safely to arrive at home.
Jesus sought me when a stranger,
  Wand'ring from the fold of God:
He, to rescue me·from danger,
  Interposed his precious blood.

3 O! to grace how great a debtor
  Daily I'm constrain'd to be !
Let thy goodness, like a fetter,
  Bind my wand'ring heart to thee:
Prone to wander, Lord, I feel it—
  Prone to leave the God I love;
Here's my heart, O take and seal it—
  Seal it for thy courts above.

8

Grateful adoration.

BEFORE Jehovah's awful throne,
　Ye nations bow with sacred joy;
Know that the Lord is God alone,—
　He can create, and he destroy.

2 His sov'reign power, without our aid,
　Made us of clay, and form'd us men;
And when like wand'ring sheep we stray'd,
　He brought us to his fold again.

3 We'll crowd thy gates with thankful songs,
　High as the heavens our voices raise;
And earth, with her ten thousand tongues,
　Shall fill thy courts with sounding praise.

4 Wide as the world is thy command;
　Vast as eternity thy love;
Firm as a rock thy truth shall stand,
　When rolling years shall cease to move.

PRAYER.

9　　　　　　　　　　　L. M.

The mercy-seat.

FROM every stormy wind that blows,
　From every swelling tide of woes,
There is a calm, a sure retreat:
'Tis found beneath the mercy-seat.

2 There is a place where Jesus sheds
The oil of gladness on our heads;
A place than all besides more sweet,—
It is the blood-bought mercy-seat.

3 Ah! whither could we flee for aid,
When tempted, desolate, dismay'd?
Or how the hosts of hell defeat,
Had suff'ring saints no mercy-seat?

4 There, there on eagles' wings we soar,
And sin and sense molest no more;
And Heaven comes down our souls to greet,
While glory crowns the mercy-seat.

10   4 lines 7s.

For a general blessing.

L ORD, we come before thee now,
At thy feet we humbly bow:
O, do not our suit disdain;
Shall we seek thee, Lord, in vain?

2 Lord, on thee our souls depend;
In compassion now descend;
Fill our hearts with thy rich grace,
Tune our lips to sing thy praise.

3 Comfort those who weep and mourn;
Let the time of joy return;
Those that are cast down lift up;
Make them strong in faith and hope.

4 Grant that all may seek and find
Thee, a gracious God and kind:
Heal the sick, the captive free;
Let us all rejoice in thee.

11

The hearer of prayer.

YE praying souls, rejoice,
 And bless your Father's Name;
With joy to him lift up your voice,
 And all his love proclaim.

2 Your mournful cry he hears;
 He marks your feeblest groan,
Supplies your wants, dispels your fears,
 And makes his mercy known.

3 To all his praying saints
 He ever will attend,
And to their sorrows and complaints
 His ear in mercy bend.

4 Then let us still go on
 In his appointed ways,
Rejoicing in his Name alone,
 In prayer and humble praise.

12

For quickening power.

COME, Holy Spirit, heavenly Dove,
 With all thy quick'ning powers;
Kindle a flame of sacred love
 In these cold hearts of ours.

2 Look how we grovel here below,
 Fond of these earthly toys;
Our souls, how heavily they go
 To reach eternal joys.

3 Father, and shall we ever live
 At this poor dying rate;
Our love so faint, so cold to thee,
 And thine to us so great?

4 Come, Holy Spirit, heavenly Dove,
  With all thy quick'ning powers;
Come, shed abroad a Saviour's love,
  And that shall kindle ours.

13   C. M.

What is prayer?

PRAYER is the soul's sincere desire,
  Utter'd or unexpress'd;
The motion of a hidden fire
  That trembles in the breast.

2 Prayer is the burden of a sigh,—
  The falling of a tear,—
The upward glancing of an eye,
  When none but God is near.

8 Prayer is the simplest form of speech
  That infant lips can try;
Prayer, the sublimest strains that reach
  The Majesty on high.

4 Prayer is the Christian's vital breath,
  The Christian's native air;
His watchword at the gates of death,—
  He enters heaven with prayer.

5 Prayer is the contrite sinner's voice,
  Returning from his ways;
While angels, in their songs, rejoice,
  And cry,—Behold, he prays!

6 O Thou, by whom we come to God,—
  The Life, the Truth, the Way,—
The path of prayer thyself hast trod:—
  Lord, teach us how to pray!

14
4 lines 7s.

Encouragements to pray.

COME, my soul, thy suit prepare;
  Jesus loves to answer prayer;
He himself invites thee near,—
Bids thee ask him, waits to hear.

2 Lord, I come to thee for rest;
Take possession of my breast;
There, thy blood-bought right maintain,
And without a rival reign.

3 While I am a pilgrim here,
Let thy love my spirit cheer;
As my guide, my guard, my friend,
Lead me to my journey's end.

4 Show me what I have to do;
Every hour my strength renew;
Let me live a life of faith,—
Let me die thy people's death.

15
S. M.

Claiming the promise.

JESUS, we look to thee,
  Thy promised presence claim;
Thou in the midst of us shalt be,
  Assembled in thy name:

2 Thy name salvation is,
  Which here we come to prove:
Thy name is life, and health, and peace,
  And everlasting love.

3 Present we know thou art,
  But O, thyself reveal!
Now, Lord, let every bounding heart
  The mighty comfort feel.

4 O may thy quick'ning voice
   The death of sin remove;
And bid our inmost souls rejoice,
   In hope of perfect love.

16   S. M.

For a revival.

O LORD, thy work revive,
   In Zion's gloomy hour,
And let our dying graces live
   By thy restoring power.

2 O let thy chosen few
   Awake to earnest prayer;
Their covenant again renew,
   And walk in filial fear.

3 Thy Spirit then will speak
   Through lips of humble clay,
Till hearts of adamant shall break,—
   Till rebels shall obey.

4 Now lend thy gracious ear;
   Now listen to our cry;
O come, and bring salvation near;
   Our souls on thee rely.

17   .   L. M.

Sweet hour of prayer.

SWEET hour of prayer, sweet hour of
   prayer,
That calls me from a world of care,
And bids me at my Father's throne
Make all my wants and wishes known:
In seasons of distress and grief
My soul has often found relief,
And oft escaped the tempter's snare
By thy return, sweet hour of prayer.

2 Sweet hour of prayer, sweet hour of prayer.
May I thy consolations share,
Till from Mount Pisgah's lofty height
I view my home and take my flight:
This robe of flesh I'll drop, and rise
To seize the everlasting prize,
And shout, while passing through the air,
Farewell, farewell, sweet hour of prayer.

AWAKENING.

18   S. M.

The horrors of the second death.

O WHERE shall rest be found,—
  Rest for the weary soul?
'Twere vain the ocean's depths to sound,
  Or pierce to either pole.

2 The world can never give
  The bliss for which we sigh;
'Tis not the whole of life to live,
  Nor all of death to die.

3 Beyond this vale of tears
  There is a life above
Unmeasured by the flight of years;
  And all that life is love.

4 There is a death, whose pang
  Outlasts the fleeting breath:
O what eternal horrors hang
  Around the second death!

5 Thou God of truth and grace!
  Teach us that death to shun;
Lest we be banish'd from thy face,
  For evermore undone.

19 C. M.
The dreadful sentence.

THAT awful day will surely come,
  The' appointed hour makes haste,
When I must stand before my Judge,
  And pass the solemn test.

2 Jesus, thou source of all my joys,
  Thou ruler of my heart,
How could I bear to hear thy voice
  Pronounce the word,—Depart!

3 What, to be banish'd from my Lord,
  And yet forbid to die;
To linger in eternal pain,
  And death forever fly!—

4 O wretched state of deep despair,
  To see my God remove,
And fix my doleful station where
  I must not taste his love.

    The judgment day is rolling on,
    The judgment day is rolling on,
    The judgment day is rolling on,
        Prepare to meet thy God.

20 4 lines 7s.
The danger of delay.

HASTEN, sinner, to be wise!
  Stay not for the morrow's sun:
Wisdom if you still despise,
  Harder is it to be won.

2 Hasten, mercy to implore !
  Stay not for the morrow's sun,
Lest thy season should be o'er
  Ere this evening's stage be run.

3 Hasten, sinner, to return !
  Stay not for the morrow's sun,
Lest thy lamp should fail to burn
  Ere salvation's work is done.

4 Hasten, sinner, to be blest !
  Stay not for the morrow's sun,
Lest perdition thee arrest
  Ere the morrow is begun.

21   886, 886.
The momentous question.

AND am I only born to die?
  And must I suddenly comply
  With nature's stern decree?
What after death for me remains?
Celestial joys, or hellish pains,
  To all eternity.

2 How then ought I on earth to live,
While God prolongs the kind reprieve,
  And props the house of clay?
My sole concern, my single care,
To watch, and tremble, and prepare
  Against that fatal day.

3 Nothing is worth a thought beneath,
But how I may escape the death
  That never, never dies !
How make mine own election sure;
And when I fail on earth, secure
  A mansion in the skies.

4 Jesus, vouchsafe a pitying ray;
Be thou my Guide, be thou my Way
  To glorious happiness.
Ah! write the pardon on my heart;
And whensoe'er I hence depart,
  Let me depart in peace.

———◆———

INVITATION.

22   87, 87, 47.

The invitation.

COME, ye sinners, poor and needy,
  Weak and wounded, sick and sore;
Jesus ready stands to save you,
  Full of pity, love, and power:
      He is able,
  He is willing: doubt no more.

2 Let not conscience make you linger;
  Nor of fitness fondly dream:
All the fitness he requireth
  Is to feel your need of him:
      This he gives you,—
  'Tis the Spirit's glimm'ring beam.

3 Come, ye weary, heavy-laden,
  Bruised and mangled by the fall;
If you tarry till you're better,
  You will never come at all;
      Not the righteous,—
  Sinners Jesus came to call.

4 Agonizing in the garden,
  Your Redeemer prostrate lies;
On the bloody tree behold him!
Hear him cry, before he dies,
  It is finished!—
Sinners, will not this suffice?

23   The gospel feast.   L. M.

COME, sinners, to the gospel feast;
  Let every soul be Jesus' guest:
Ye need not one be left behind,
For God hath bidden all mankind.

2 Sent by my Lord, on you I call;
The invitation is to all:—
Come all the world! come, sinner, thou!
All things in Christ are ready now.

3 Come, all ye souls by sin oppress'd,
Ye restless wand'rers after rest;
Ye poor, and maim'd, and halt, and blind,
In Christ a hearty welcome find.

4 See him set forth before your eyes,
That precious, bleeding sacrifice:
His offer'd benefits embrace,
And freely now be saved by grace.

24   Will you go?   8s, 3s.

WE'RE trav'ling home to heaven above:
     Will you go?
To sing the Saviour's dying love:
     Will you go?
Millions have reached that blest abode,
Anointed kings and priests to God,
And millions more are on the road:
     Will you go?

2 We're going to walk the plains of light :
　　　　　　Will you go?
Far, far from death and curse and night:
　　　　　　Will you go?
The crown of life we then shall wear,
The conqueror's palm we then shall bear,
And all the joys of heaven we'll share:
　　　　　　Will you go?

3 The way to heaven is straight and plain:
　　　　　　Will you go?
Repent, believe, be born again!
　　　　　　Will you go?
The Saviour cries aloud to thee,
" Take up thy cross and follow me,
And thou shalt my salvation see:"
　　　　　　Will you go?

4 O! could I hear some sinner say,
　　　　　　I will go!
I'll start this moment, clear the way;
　　　　　　Let me go.
My old companions, fare you well,
I will not go with you to hell,
I mean with Jesus Christ to dwell.
　　　　　　Let me go.

25　　　　　　C. M.
The resolution.

COME, humble sinner, in whose breast
　A thousand thoughts revolve;
Come, with your guilt and fear oppress'd,
　And make this last resolve:—

2 I'll go to Jesus, though my sin
　Like mountains round me close;
I know his courts, I'll enter in,
　Whatever may oppose.

3 Prostrate I'll lie before his throne,
  And there my guilt confess; .
I'll tell him I'm a wretch undone
Without his sov'reign grace.

4 Perhaps he will admit my plea,
  Perhaps will hear my prayer;
But, if I perish, I will pray,
And perish only there.

5 I can but perish if I go—
  I am resolved to try;
For if I stay away, I know
I must forever die.

26   11, 10, 11, 10.
Earth has no sorrow that Heaven cannot heal.

COME, ye disconsolate, where'er ye lan-
      guish;
  Come to the mercy-seat, fervently kneel;
Here bring your wounded hearts, here tell
      your anguish;—
  Earth has no sorrow that Heaven cannot
      heal.

2 Joy of the desolate, light of the straying,
  Hope of the penitent, fadeless and pure,—
Here speaks the Comforter, tenderly say-
      ing,—
  Earth has no sorrow that heaven cannot
      cure.

27   S. M.
All-sufficient grace.

GRACE! 'tis a charming sound,
  Harmonious to the ear;
Heaven with the echo shall resound,
And all the earth shall hear.

2 Grace taught my roving feet
  To tread the heavenly road;
And new supplies each hour I meet
  While pressing on to God.

3 Grace all the work shall crown,
  Through everlasting days;
It lays in heaven the topmost stone,
  And well deserves our praise.

CHORUS.

I'm glad salvation's free;
I'm glad salvation's free;
Salvation's free for you and me;
I'm glad salvation's free.

28   4 6s & 2 8s.

The jubilee trumpet.

BLOW ye the trumpet, blow
  The gladly-solemn sound;
Let all the nations know,
  To earth's remotest bound,
The year of jubilee is come;
Return, ye ransom'd sinners, home.

2 Jesus, our great High Priest,
  Hath full atonement made:
Ye weary spirits, rest;
  Ye mournful souls be glad:
The year of jubilee is come;
Return, ye ransom'd sinners, home.

3 Extol the Lamb of God,—
  The all-atoning Lamb;
Redemption in his blood
  Throughout the world proclaim:
The year of jubilee is come;
Return, ye ransom'd sinners, home.

29
S. M.

Embracing the all-sufficient portion.

A ND can I yet delay
My little all to give?
To tear my soul from earth away
For Jesus to receive?

2 Nay, but I yield, I yield;
I can hold out no more:
I sink, by dying love compell'd,
And own thee conqueror.

3 Though late, I all forsake;
My friends, my all, resign:
Gracious Redeemer, take, O take,
And seal me ever thine.

4 Come, and possess me whole,
Nor hence again remove;
Settle and fix my wav'ring soul
With all thy weight of love.

5 My life, my portion thou;
Thou all-sufficient art:
My hope, my heavenly treasure, now
Enter, and keep my heart.

30

Mercy's free.

B Y faith I view my Saviour dying
On the tree, on the tree;
To every nation he is crying,
Look on me, look on me.
He bids the guilty now draw near,
Repent, believe, dismiss their fear—
Hark! hark! what precious words I hear,
Mercy's free, mercy's free.

2 Did Christ, when I was sin pursuing,
  Pity me, pity me,
And did he snatch my soul from ruin,
  Can it be, can it be?
O yes, he did salvation bring,
He is my prophet, priest, and king,
And now my happy soul can sing,
  Mercy's free, mercy's free.

3 Jesus my weary soul refreshes—
  Mercy's free, mercy's free.
And every moment Christ is precious
  Unto me, unto me.
None can describe the bliss I prove,
While through the wilderness I rove,
All may enjoy the Saviour's love—
  Mercy's free, mercy's free.

4 Long as I live I'll still be crying,
  Mercy's free, mercy's free.
And this shall be my theme when dying,
  Mercy's free, mercy's free.
And when the vale of death I've passed,
When lodged above the stormy blast,
I'll sing, while endless ages last,
  Mercy's free, mercy's free.

31
Come to Jesus.

COME to Jesus,
  He will save you,
He is willing;
I believe it.
Can you doubt him;
See him pleading—
Lo, he saves you—
  Halleluiah!   Amen.

Just now.

PENITENTIAL.

32 *   L. M.

Just as I am.

JUST as I am—without one plea,
But that thy blood was shed for me,
And that thou bidd'st me come to thee,
    O Lamb of God, I come!

2 Just as I am—and waiting not
To rid my soul of one dark blot,
To thee, whose blood can cleanse each spot,
    O Lamb of God, I come!

3 Just as I am—though tossed about
With many a conflict, many a doubt—
"Fightings within, and fears without,"
    O Lamb of God, I come!

4 Just as I am—poor, wretched, blind—
Sight, riches, healing of the mind,
Yea, all I need, in thee to find:
    O Lamb of God, I come!

5 Just as I am—thou wilt receive,
Wilt welcome, pardon, cleanse, relieve,
Because thy promise I believe:
    O Lamb of God, I come!

6 Just as I am—thy love, I own,
Has broken every barrier down;
Now, to be thine, yea, thine alone,
    O Lamb of God, I come!

33

L. M.

Deprecating the withdrawal of the Spirit.

STAY, thou insulted Spirit, stay,
  Though I have done thee such despite;
Nor cast the sinner quite away,
  Nor take thine everlasting flight.

2 Though I have steel'd my stubborn heart,
  And shaken off my guilty fears;
And vex'd, and urged thee to depart,
  For many long rebellious years:

3 Yet, O! the chief of sinners spare,
  In honor of my great High Priest;
Nor in thy righteous anger swear
  To' exclude me from thy people's rest.

34

8 lines 7s.

The only refuge.

JESUS, lover of my soul,
  Let me to thy bosom fly,
While the nearer waters roll,
  While the tempest still is high;
Hide me, O my Saviour, hide,
  Till the storm of life is past;
Safe into the haven guide,
  O receive my soul at last.

2 Other refuge have I none;
  Hangs my helpless soul on thee:
Leave, O leave me not alone;
  Still support and comfort me:
All my trust on thee is stay'd;
  All my help from thee I bring;
Cover my defenseless head
  With the shadow of thy wing.

3 Thou, O Christ, art all I want:
  More than all in thee I find :
Raise the fallen, cheer the faint,
  Heal the sick, and lead the blind.
Just and holy is thy name;
  I am all unrighteousness;
False, and full of sin I am;
  Thou art full of truth and grace.

35　　　　　　　　　　C. M.

Godly sorrow at the cross.

ALAS! and did my Saviour bleed?
  And did my Sov'reign die?
Would he devote that sacred head
  For such a worm as I?

2 Was it for crimes that I have done
  He groan'd upon the tree?
Amazing pity! grace unknown!
  And love beyond degree!

3 Thus might I hide my blushing face
  While his dear cross appears;
Dissolve my heart in thankfulness,
  And melt mine eyes to tears.

4 But drops of grief can ne'er repay
  The debt of love I owe:
Here, Lord, I give myself away,—
  'Tis all that I can do.

CHORUS.

O Jesus! dear Saviour, we look to thee—
Remember, Lord, thy dying groans,
  And then remember me.

36   L. M.
The light yoke and easy burden.

O THAT my load of sin were gone;
  O that I could at last submit
At Jesus' feet to lay it down—
  To lay my soul at Jesus' feet.

2 Rest for my soul I long to find:
  Saviour of all, if mine thou art,
Give me thy meek and lowly mind,
  And stamp thine image on my heart.

3 Break off the yoke of inbred sin,
  And fully set my spirit free; .
I cannot rest till pure within,—
  Till I am wholly lost in thee.

4 I would, but thou must give the power
  My heart from every sin release;
Bring near, bring near the joyful hour,
  And fill me with thy perfect peace.

37   4 lines 7s.
Mercy for the chief of sinners.

DEPTH of mercy! can there be
  Mercy still reserved for me?
Can my God his wrath forbear?
Me, the chief of sinners, spare?

2 I have long withstood his grace;
Long provoked him to his face;
Would not hearken to his calls;
Grieved him by a thousand falls.

3 Now incline me to repent;
Let me now my sins lament;
Now my foul revolt deplore,
Weep, believe, and sin no more.

4 Kindled his relentings are;
Me he now delights to spare;
Cries, How shall I give thee up?—
Lets the lifted thunder drop.

5 There for me the Saviour stands;
Shows his wounds, and spreads his hands;
God is love! I know, I feel;
Jesus weeps, and loves me still.

CHORUS.

God is love! I know, I feel;
Jesus weeps, and loves me still.
Jesus weeps—he weeps and loves me still.

38   6 lines 7s.
Clinging to the Cross.

ROCK of ages, cleft for me,
  Let me hide myself in thee;
Let the water and the blood,
From thy wounded side which flow'd,
Be of sin the double cure,—
Save from wrath and make me pure.

2 Could my tears forever flow,—
Could my zeal no languor know,—
These for sin could not atone;
Thou must save, and thou alone:
In my hand no price I bring;
Simply to the cross I cling.

3 While I draw this fleeting breath,
When my eyes shall close in death,
When I rise to worlds unknown,
And behold thee on thy throne,—
Rock of ages, cleft for me,
Let me hide myself in thee.

39
Unwearied earnestness. C. M.

FATHER, I stretch my hands to thee;
 No other help I know:
If thou withdraw thyself from me,
 Ah! whither shall I go?

CHORUS.

I yield, I yield, I yield,
 I can hold out no more.

2 Author of faith! to thee I lift
 My weary, longing eyes:
O let me now receive that gift,—
 My soul without it dies.

3 Surely, thou canst not let me die;
 O speak, and I shall live;
And here I will unwearied lie,
 Till thou thy Spirit give.

4 How would my fainting soul rejoice,
 Could I but see thy face;
Now let me hear thy quick'ning voice,
 And taste thy pard'ning grace.

40
Humility and contrition. 76, 76, 78, 76.

JESUS, let thy pitying eye
 Call back a wand'ring sheep;
False to thee, like Peter, I
 Would fain like Peter weep.
Let me be by grace restored;
 On me be all long-suff'ring shown:
Turn, and look upon me, Lord,
 And break my heart of stone.

2 Saviour, Prince, enthroned above,
  Repentance to impart,
Give me, through thy dying love,
  The humble contrite heart:
Give what I have long implored,
  A portion of thy grief unknown:
Turn, and look upon me, Lord,
  And break my heart of stone.

41
S. M

Waiting at the Cross.

FATHER, I dare believe
  Thee merciful and true:
Thou wilt my guilty soul forgive,—
  My fallen soul renew.

2 Come, then, for Jesus' sake,
  And bid my heart be clean;
An end of all my troubles make,—
  An end of all my sin.

3 I cannot wash my heart,
  But by believing thee,
And waiting for thy blood to' impart
  The spotless purity.

4 While at thy cross I lie,
  Jesus, the grace bestow;
Now thy all-cleansing blood apply,
  And I am white as snow.

42
L. M

Condemned, but pleading the promises.

SHOW pity, Lord; O Lord, forgive;
  Let a repenting rebel live.
Are not thy mercies large and free?
May not a sinner trust in thee?

2 My crimes are great, but don't surpass
The power and glory of thy grace;
Great God, thy nature hath no bound,
So let thy pard'ning love be found.

3 O wash my soul from every sin,
And make my guilty conscience clean;
Here on my heart the burden lies,
And past offenses pain my eyes.

4 O save a trembling sinner, Lord,
Whose hope, still hov'ring round thy Word,
Would light on some sweet promise there,—
Some sure support against despair.

43   6 lines 8s.

Wrestling Jacob: I will not let thee go.

COME, O thou Traveler unknown,
  Whom still I hold, but cannot see;
My company before is gone,
  And I am left alone with thee:
With thee all night I mean to stay,
And wrestle till the break of day.

2 I need not tell thee who I am;
  My sin and misery declare;
Thyself hast call'd me by my name;
  Look on thy hands, and read it there:
But who, I ask thee, who art thou?
Tell me thy name, and tell me now.

3 What though my shrinking flesh complain,
  And murmur to contend so long?
I rise superior to my pain:
  When I am weak, then I am strong!
And when my all of strength shall fail,
I shall with the God-man prevail.

44   C. M.

Lamenting the absence of the Spirit.

O FOR a closer walk with God,—
  A calm and heavenly frame;
A light to shine upon the road
That leads me to the Lamb.

2 Where is the blessedness I knew,
  When first I saw the Lord?
Where is the soul-refreshing view
Of Jesus and his Word?

3 Return, O holy Dove, return,
  Sweet messenger of rest;
I hate the sins that made thee mourn,
  And drove thee from my breast. .

4 The dearest idol I have known,
  Whate'er that idol be,
Help me to tear it from thy throne,
And worship only thee.

5 So shall my walk be close with God,
  Calm and serene my frame;
So purer light shall mark the road
  That leads me to the Lamb.

45   7s, 6s, & 8s.

The Cross.

BEHOLD! behold! the Lamb of God,
  On the cross, on the cross!
For you he shed his precious blood,
  On the cross, on the cross!
The rocks do rend, the mountains quake,
While Jesus doth atonement make—
While Jesus suffers for our sake,
  On the cross, on the cross.

2 Come, sinners, see him lifted up,
   On the cross, on the cross!
He drinks for you the bitter cup,
   On the cross, on the cross!
To heaven he turns his languid eyes:
"'Tis finish'd!" now the Conqu'ror cries,
Then bows his sacred head and dies,
   On the cross, on the cross!

3 Where'er I go I'll tell the story
   Of the cross, of the cross!
In nothing else my soul shall glory,
   Save the cross, save the cross!
Yes, this my constant theme shall be,
Through time and in eternity,
That Jesus suffer'd death for me,
   On the cross, on the cross!

4 Let every mourner come and cling
   To the cross, to the cross!
Let every Christian come and sing,
   Round the cross, round the cross!
Here let the preacher take his stand,
And with the Bible in his hand,
Proclaim the triumphs of the Lamb
   On the cross, on the cross!

CONVERSION.
46   **L. M.**
The highway of holiness.

JESUS, my all, to heaven is gone,—
   He, whom I fix my hopes upon:
His track I see, and I'll pursue
The narrow way, till him I view.

2 The way the holy prophets went,—
The road that leads from banishment,—
The King's highway of holiness,
I'll go, for all his paths are peace.

3 This is the way I long have sought,
And mourn'd because I found it not;
My grief a burden long has been,
Because I was not saved from sin.

4 The more I strove against its power,
I felt its weight and guilt the more;
Till late I heard my Saviour say,—
Come hither, soul, I am the way.

5 Lo! glad I come; and thou, blest Lamb,
Shalt take me to thee, as I am:
Nothing but sin have I to give,—
Nothing but love shall I receive.

6 Then will I tell to sinners round,
What a dear Saviour I have found!
I'll point to thy redeeming blood,
And say,—Behold the way to God!

47   L. M.
Vows remembered and renewed.

O HAPPY day that fix'd my choice
On thee, my Saviour and my God!
Well may this glowing heart rejoice,
And tell its raptures all abroad.

CHORUS.

Happy day, happy day,
When Jesus washed my sins away;
He taught me how to watch and pray,
And live rejoicing every day.
Happy day, happy day,
When Jesus washed my sins away.

2 'Tis done—the great transaction's done;
  I am my Lord's, and he is mine;
He drew me and I follow'd on,
  Charmed to confess the voice divine.

3 Now rest, my long-divided heart;
  Fix'd on this blissful center, rest;
Nor ever from thy Lord depart:
  With him of every good possess'd.

48   **12 9, 12 9.**
Joy of the young convert.

O HOW happy are they
  Who the Saviour obey,
And have laid up their treasure above;
  Tongue can never express
  The sweet comfort and peace
Of a soul in its earliest love.

2 That sweet comfort was mine,
  When the favor divine
I received through the blood of the Lamb;
  When my heart first believed
  What a joy I received,—
What a heaven in Jesus's name!

3 'Twas a heaven below
  My Redeemer to know,
And the angels could do nothing more
  Than to fall at his feet
  And the story repeat,
And the Lover of sinners adore.

4 Jesus all the day long
  Was my joy and my song:
O that all his salvation might see!
  He hath loved me, I cried;
  He hath suffer'd and died,
To redeem even rebels like me.

49   4 6s & 2 8s.
"Abba, Father."

A RISE, my soul, arise;
  Shake off thy guilty fears;
The bleeding Sacrifice
  In my behalf appears:
Before the throne my Surety stands;
My name is written on his hands.

2 Five bleeding wounds he bears,
  Received on Calvary;
They pour effectual prayers,
  They strongly plead for me:—
Forgive him, O forgive, they cry,
Nor let that ransom'd sinner die.

3 The Father hears him pray,
  His dear anointed One:
He cannot turn away
  The presence of his Son:
His Spirit answers to the blood,
And tells me I am born of God.

4 My God is reconciled;
  His pard'ning voice I hear:
He owns me for his child;
  I can no longer fear:
With confidence I now draw nigh,
And Father, Abba, Father, cry.

50
          Finding Salvation.

I HAVE sought round the verdant earth
  For unfading joy;
I have tried every source of mirth,
  But all, all will cloy.

Lord, bestow on me
Grace to set the spirit free;
Thine the praise shall be;
  Mine, mine the joy.

2 I have wander'd in mazes dark
  Of doubt and distress,
I have had not a kindling spark
  My spirit to bless;
Cheerless unbelief
Filled my lab'ring soul with grief.
What shall give relief?
  What shall give peace?

3 I then turned to thy Gospel, Lord,
  From folly away;
I then trusted thy holy Word
  That taught me to pray.
Here I found release—
Weary spirit here found rest;
Hope of endless bliss,
  Eternal day.

4 I will praise now my heavenly King,
  I'll praise and adore;
The heart's richest tribute bring
  To Thee, God of power;
And in heaven above,
Saved by thy redeeming love,
Loud the strains shall move
  For evermore.

51   L. M.
Love which passeth knowledge.

OF Him who did salvation bring
  I could forever think and sing;
Arise, ye needy,—he'll relieve;
Arise, ye guilty,—he'll forgive.

2 Ask but his grace, and lo, 'tis given;
Ask, and he turns your hell to heaven:
Though sin and sorrow wound my soul,
Jesus, thy balm will make it whole.

3 To shame our sins he blush'd in blood;
He closed his eyes to show us God:
Let all the world fall down and know
That none but God such love can show.

4 Insatiate to this spring I fly;
I drink, and yet am ever dry:
Ah! who against thy charms is proof?
Ah! who that loves can love enough?

52   87, 87, 47.
Hallelujah.

O THOU God of my salvation,
  My Redeemer from all sin;
Moved by thy divine compassion,
  Who hast died my heart to win,
    I will praise thee:
  Where shall I thy praise begin?

2 Though unseen, I love the Saviour;
  He hath brought salvation near;
Manifests his pard'ning favor;
  And when Jesus doth appear,
    Soul and body
  Shall his glorious image bear.

3 While the angel choirs are crying,—
  Glory to the great I AM,
I with them will still be vying—
  Glory! glory to the Lamb!
    O how precious
  Is the sound of Jesus' name!

4 Angels now are hov'ring round us,
 Unperceived amid the throng;
Wond'ring at the love that crown'd us,
 Glad to join the holy song:
  Halleluiah,
 Love and praise to Christ belong!

53 L. M.
Because He liveth I shall live also.

I KNOW that my Redeemer lives—
 What joy the blest assurance gives!
He lives, he lives, who once was dead;
He lives, my everlasting Head!

2 He lives, to bless me with his love;
He lives, to plead for me above;
He lives, my hungry soul to feed;
He lives, to help in time of need.

3 He lives, and grants me daily breath;
He lives, and I shall conquer death;
He lives, my mansion to prepare;
He lives, to bring me safely there.

4 He lives—all glory to his name;
He lives, my Saviour, still the same;
What joy the blest assurance gives,—
I know that my Redeemer lives.

54 C. M.
Efficacy of the atoning blood.

THERE is a fountain fill'd with blood,
 Drawn from Immanuel's veins;
And sinners, plunged beneath that flood,
 Lose all their guilty stains.

2 The dying thief rejoiced to see
  That fountain in his day;
And there may I, though vile as he,
  Wash all my sins away.

3 Thou dying Lamb! thy precious blood
  Shall never lose its power,
Till all the ransom'd Church of God
  Are saved, to sin no more.

4 E'er since, by faith, I saw the stream
  Thy flowing wounds supply,
Redeeming love has been my theme,
  And shall be, till I die.

5 Then in a nobler, sweeter song,
  I'll sing thy power to save,
When this poor lisping, stamm'ring tongue
  Lies silent in the grave.

CHORUS.

O the Lamb, the loving Lamb,
  The Lamb on Calvary;
The Lamb that was slain, but lives again,
  To intercede for me.

55   C. M.
The precious Name.

HOW sweet the name of Jesus sounds
  In a believer's ear;
It soothes his sorrows, heals his wounds,
  And drives away his fear.

2 It makes the wounded spirit whole,
  And calms the troubled breast;
'Tis manna to the hungry soul,
  And to the weary, rest.

3 Dear Name, the rock on which I build,
   My shield and hiding-place;
My never-failing-treasure, fill'd
   With boundless stores of grace;

4 Jesus, my Shepherd, Saviour, Friend,
   My Prophet, Priest, and King,
My Lord, my Life, my Way, my End,
   Accept the praise I bring.

5 I would thy boundless love proclaim
   With every fleeting breath;
So shall the music of thy name
   Refresh my soul in death.

CHORUS.

O who's like Jesus—halleluiah!
   Praise ye the Lord;
There's none like Jesus—halleluiah!
   Love and serve the Lord.

56
Love for Jesus.

I LOVE thee, I love thee, I love thee my
   Lord,
I love thee, my Saviour, I love thee, my
   God;
I love thee, I love thee, and that thou dost
   know,
But how much I love thee I never can
   show.

2 I'm happy, I'm happy, O wondrous ac-
   count!
My joys are immortal, I stand on the
   Mount!
I gaze on my treasure, and long to be there
With Jesus and angels, my kindred so dear.

3 O Jesus, my Saviour, with thee I am blest!
My life and salvation, my joy and my rest!
Thy name be my theme, and thy love be
    my song,
Thy grace shall inspire both my heart and
    my tongue.

57   7s & 6s.
Cheer for drooping souls.

DROOPING souls, no longer grieve,
    Heaven is propitious ;
If in Christ you now believe,
    You will find him precious.
Jesus now is passing by,
    Calling mourners to him ;
He has died, you need not die,
    Now look up and view him.

2 He has pardons, full and free,
    Drooping souls to gladden ;
Jesus calls, "Come unto me,"
    Weary, heavy laden.
Though your sins like mountains rise,
    Rise, and reach to heaven ;
Soon as you on him rely,
    All shall be forgiven.

3 Streaming mercy, how it flows,
    Now I know, I feel it ;
Half has never yet been told,
    Yet I want to tell it.
Jesus' blood has heal'd my wound,
    O, the wondrous story !
I was lost, but now am found,
    Glory ! Glory ! Glory !

58

The spot where I was converted.

THERE is a spot, to me more dear
  Than native vale or mountain—
A spot, for which affection's tear
  Springs, grateful, from its fountain:
'Tis not where kindred souls abound,
  Though that on earth were heaven;
But where I first my Saviour found,
  And felt my sins forgiven!

2 Hard was my toil to reach the shore—
  Long lost upon the ocean;
Above me was the thunder's roar,—
  Beneath, the waves' commotion:
Darkly the pall of night was thrown
  Around me, faint with terror;
In that dark hour, how did my groan
  Ascend, for years of error!

3 Sinking and panting, as for breath,
  I knew not help was near me;
I cried, O save me, Lord, from death!
  Immortal Jesus, hear me!
Then, quick as thought, I felt him mine;
  My Saviour stood before me:
I saw His brightness round me shine,
  And shouted, Glory! Glory!

4 O happy hour! O hallow'd spot!
  Where love divine first found me;
Wherever falls my distant lot,
  My heart shall linger round thee:
And when from earth I rise to soar
  Up to my home in heaven,
Down will I cast my eyes once more
  Where I was first forgiven.

HOLINESS.

59 C. M.

Entire purification.

FOREVER here my rest shall be,
  Close to thy bleeding side;
This all my hope, and all my plea,—
  For me the Saviour died.

2 My dying Saviour, and my God,
  Fountain for guilt and sin,
Sprinkle me ever with thy blood,
  And cleanse and keep me clean.

3 Wash me, and make me thus thine own;
  Wash me, and mine thou art;
Wash me, but not my feet alone,—
  My hands, my head, my heart.

4 The' atonement of thy blood apply,
  Till faith to sight improve;
Till hope in full fruition die,
  And all my soul be love.

CHORUS.

I will believe, I do believe,
  That Jesus died for me;
And through his blood, his precious blood,
  I shall from sin be free.

60 C. M.

Renewing the covenant.

COME, let us use the grace divine,
  And all, with one accord,
In a perpetual cov'nant join
  Ourselves to Christ the Lord;—

2 Give up ourselves, through Jesus' power,
  His name to glorify;
And promise, in this sacred hour,
  For God to live and die.

3 The cov'nant we this moment make
  Be ever kept in mind;
We will no more our God forsake,
  Or cast his words behind.

4 We never will throw off his fear,
  Who hears our solemn vow;
And if thou art well pleased to hear,
  Come down and meet us now.

5 Thee, Father, Son, and Holy Ghost,
  Let all our hearts receive;
Present with the celestial host,
  The peaceful answer give.

6 To each the cov'nant blood apply,
  Which takes our sins away;
And register our names on high,
  And keep us to that day.

61   **L. M.**

Thirsting for the fullness of love.

I THIRST, thou wounded Lamb of God,
  To wash me in thy cleansing blood;
To dwell within thy wounds; then pain
Is sweet, and life or death is gain.

2 Take my poor heart, and let it be
Forever closed to all but thee:
Seal thou my breast, and let me wear
That pledge of love forever there.

3 How blest are they who still abide
Close shelter'd in thy bleeding side!
Who thence their life and strength derive,
And by thee move, and in thee live.

4 How can it be, thou heavenly King,
That thou shouldst us to glory bring;
Make slaves the partners of thy throne,
Deck'd with a never-fading crown?

5 Hence our hearts melt, our eyes o'erflow,
Our words are lost, nor will we know,
Nor will we think of aught beside,—
My Lord, my Love, is crucified.

62 C. M.

The refining fire of the Holy Spirit.

JESUS, thine all-victorious love
  Shed in my heart abroad:
Then shall my feet no longer rove,
  Rooted and fix'd in God.

2 O that in me the sacred fire
  Might now begin to glow;
Burn up the dross of base desire,
  And make the mountains flow.

3 O that it now from heaven might fall,
  And all my sins consume:
Come, Holy Ghost, for thee I call;
  Spirit of burning, come.

4 Refining fire, go through my heart;
  Illuminate my soul;
Scatter thy life through every part,
  And sanctify the whole.

63
L. M.

The vow sealed at the Cross.

LORD, I am thine, entirely thine,
Purchased and saved by blood divine;
With full consent thine I would be,
And own thy sov'reign right in me.

2 Thine would I live—thine would I die;
Be thine through all eternity;
The vow is past beyond repeal,
And now I set the solemn seal.

3 Here, at that cross where flows the blood
That bought my guilty soul for God,—
Thee, my new Master, now I call,
And consecrate to thee my all.

4 Do thou assist a feeble worm
The great engagement to perform;
Thy grace can full assistance lend,
And on that grace I dare depend.

64
S. M.

Glorious liberty.

O COME, and dwell in me,
Spirit of power within;
And bring the glorious liberty
From sorrow, fear, and sin?

2 I want the witness, Lord,
That all I do is right,—
According to thy will and word,—
Well pleasing in thy sight.

3 I ask no higher state;
Indulge me but in this,
And soon or later then translate
To my eternal bliss.

4

65 C. M.

A perfect heart the Redeemer's throne.

O FOR a heart to praise my God,
　A heart from sin set free ;—
A heart that always feels thy blood,
　So freely spill'd for me :—

2 A heart resigned, submissive, meek,
　My great Redeemer's throne ;
Where only Christ is heard to speak,—
　Where Jesus reigns alone.

3 O for a lowly, contrite heart,
　Believing, true, and clean ;
Which neither life nor death can part
　From Him that dwells within :—

4 A heart in every thought renew'd,
　And full of love divine ;
Perfect, and right, and pure, and good,—
　A copy, Lord, of thine.

66 886, 886.

Panting after the fullness of love.

O LOVE divine, how sweet thou art !
　When shall I find my willing heart
　　All taken up by thee?
I thirst, I faint, I die to prove
The greatness of redeeming love,—
　The love of Christ to me.

2 God only knows the love of God ;
O that it now were shed abroad
　In this poor stony heart :
For love I sigh, for love I pine ;
This only portion, Lord, be mine ;
　Be mine this better part.

3 O that I could forever sit
With Mary at the Master's feet!
  Be this my happy choice;
My only care, delight, and bliss,
My joy, my heaven on earth, be this,
  To hear the Bridegroom's voice.

4 O that I could, with favor'd John,
Recline my weary head upon
  The dear Redeemer's breast:
From care, and sin, and sorrow free,
Give me, O Lord, to find in thee
  My everlasting rest.

67   C. M.

Longing to be dissolved in love.

JESUS hath died that I might live,
  Might live to God alone;
In him eternal life receive,
  And be in spirit one.

2 My soul breaks out in strong desire
  The perfect bliss to prove;
My longing heart is all on fire
  To be dissolved in love.

3 Give me thyself; from every boast,
  From every wish set free;
Let all I am in thee be lost,
  But give thyself to me.

4 Thy gifts, alas! cannot suffice,
  Unless thyself be given;
Thy presence makes my paradise,
  And where thou art is heaven.

68   664, 6664.

For the Saviour's guidance.

MY faith looks up to thee,
  Thou Lamb of Calvary:
   Saviour divine,
Now hear me while I pray;
Take all my guilt away;
O let me, from this day,
   Be wholly thine.

2 May thy rich grace impart
Strength to my fainting heart;
   My zeal inspire;
As thou hast died for me,
O may my love to thee
Pure, warm, and changeless be—
   A living fire.

3 While life's dark maze I tread,
And griefs around me spread,
   Be thou my Guide:
Bid darkness turn to day;
Wipe sorrow's tears away,
Nor let me ever stray
   From thee aside.

4 When ends life's transient dream;
When death's cold, sullen stream
   Shall o'er me roll; .
Blest Saviour, then, in love,
Fear and distress remove;
O, bear me safe above,—
   A ransom'd soul.

69 6s & 4s.

Nearer, my God, to thee.

NEARER, my God, to thee,
  Nearer to thee!
E'en though it be a cross
  That raiseth me!
Still all my song shall be,
Nearer, my God, to thee,
  Nearer to thee!

2 Though like the wanderer,
  The sun gone down,
Darkness be over me,
  My rest a stone;
Yet in my dreams I'd be
Nearer, my God, to thee,
  Nearer to thee!

3 Then, with my waking thoughts
  Bright with thy praise,
Out of my stony griefs
  Bethel I'll raise;
So by my woes to be
Nearer, my God, to thee,
  Nearer to thee!

4 Or if on joyful wing
  Cleaving the sky,
Sun, moon, and stars forgot,
  Upward I fly,
Still all my song shall be—
Nearer, my God, to thee,
  Nearer to thee!

70

Thy will be done.

MY God, my Father, while I stray
Far from my home, on life's rough way,
O! teach me from my heart to say,
"Thy will be done."

2 If Thou should'st call me to resign
What most I prize,—it ne'er was mine;
I only yield Thee what was thine;—
"Thy will be done."

3 E'en if again I ne'er should see
The friend more dear than life to me,
Ere long we both shall be with Thee;—
"Thy will be done."

4 Should pining sickness waste away
My life in premature decay,
My Father, still I strive to say,
"Thy will be done."

5 If but my fainting heart be blest
With Thy sweet Spirit for its guest,
My God, to thee I leave the rest,—
"Thy will be done."

6 Renew my will from day to day,
Blend it with Thine, and take away
All that now makes it hard to say,
"Thy will be done."

7 Then when on earth I breathe no more
The prayer oft mixed with tears before,
I'll sing upon a happier shore,
"Thy will be done."

71
76, 76, 78, 76.

Determined to know nothing but Jesus, and him crucified.

VAIN, delusive world, adieu,
  With all of creature good:
Only Jesus I pursue,
  Who bought me with his blood:
All thy pleasures I forego;
  I trample on thy wealth and pride;
Only Jesus will I know,
  And Jesus crucified.

2 Here will I set up my rest;
  My fluctuating heart
From the haven of his breast
  Shall never more depart:
Whither should a sinner go?
  His wounds for me stand open wide:
Only Jesus will I know,
  And Jesus crucified.

3 Him to know is life and peace,
  And pleasure without end;
That is all my happiness,
  On Jesus to depend;
Daily in his grace to grow,
  And ever in his faith abide;
Only Jesus will I know,
  And Jesus crucified.

72
C. M.

For victorious faith.

O FOR a faith that will not shrink,
  Though press'd by every foe;
That will not tremble on the brink
  Of any earthly woe;—

2 That will not murmur nor complain
  Beneath the chast'ning rod,
But, in the hour of grief or pain,
  Will lean upon its God;—

3 A faith that shines more bright and clear
  When tempests rage without;
That when in danger knows no fear,
  In darkness feels no doubt;—

4 Lord, give us such a faith as this,
  And then, whate'er may come,
We'll taste, e'en here, the hallow'd bliss
  Of an eternal home.

73   87, 87, 87, 87.

The new creation.

LOVE divine, all love excelling,
  Joy of heaven, to earth come down,
Fix in us thy humble dwelling;
  All thy faithful mercies crown.
Jesus, thou art all compassion,—
  Pure unbounded love thou art:
Visit us with thy salvation;
  Enter every trembling heart.

2 Breathe, O breathe thy loving Spirit
  Into every troubled breast;
Let us all in thee inherit;
  Let us find that second rest.
Take away our bent to sinning;
  Alpha and Omega be;
End of faith, as its beginning,
  Set our hearts at liberty.

3 Finish then thy new creation;
　Pure and spotless let us be;
Let us see thy great salvation,
　Perfectly restored in thee:
Changed from glory into glory,
　Till in heaven we take our place,—
Till we cast our crowns before thee,
　Lost in wonder, love, and praise.

74　　　　　8s, 7s, & 4s.
"My son, give me thine heart."

WELCOME, welcome, dear Redeemer,
　Welcome to this heart of mine:
Lord, I make a full surrender,
　Every power and thought be thine;
　　Thine entirely,
Through eternal ages thine.

2 Known to all to be thy mansion,
　Earth and hell will disappear;
Or in vain attempt possession,
　When they find the Lord is near:
　　Shout, O Zion!
Shout, ye saints, the Lord is here!

CHRISTIAN LIFE.

75　　　　　C. M.
Faith sees the final triumph.

AM I a soldier of the cross,—
　A foll'wer of the Lamb,—
And shall I fear to own his cause,
　Or blush to speak his name?

2 Are there no foes for me to face?
  Must I not stem the flood?
Is this vile world a friend to grace,
  To help me on to God?

3 Since I must fight if I would reign,
  Increase my courage, Lord;
I'll bear the toil, endure the pain,
  Supported by thy word.

4 Thy saints in all this glorious war
  Shall conquer, though they die;
They see the triumph from afar,—
  By faith they bring it nigh.

76   10, 5, 11.
Renewed fidelity and zeal.

COME, let us anew our journey pursue,
  Roll round with the year,
And never stand still till the Master appear.
His adorable will let us gladly fulfill,
    And our talents improve,
By the patience of hope, and the labor of
      love.

2 O that each, in the day of his coming, may
      say,—
  I have fought my way through;
I have finished the work thou didst give
      me to do.
O that each from his Lord may receive the
      glad word,—
  Well and faithfully done!
Enter into my joy, and sit down on my
      throne.

77 S. M.

For diligence and watchfulness.

A CHARGE to keep I have,
A God to glorify;
A never-dying soul to save,
And fit it for the sky.
To serve the present age,
My calling to fulfill,—
O may it all my powers engage,
To do my Master's will.

2 Arm me with jealous care,
As in thy sight to live;
And O, thy servant, Lord, prepare,
A strict account to give.
Help me to watch and pray,
And on thyself rely,
Assured, if I my trust betray,
I shall forever die.

78 10 10, 11 11.

The Lord will provide.

THOUGH troubles assail, and dangers af-
fright,
Though friends should all fail, and foes all
unite,
Yet one thing secures us, whatever betide,
The promise assures us,—The Lord will
provide.

2 No strength of our own, nor goodness we
claim:
Our trust is all thrown on Jesus's Name;
In this our strong tower for safety we hide;
The Lord is our power,—The Lord will
provide.

3 When life sinks apace, and death is in
    view,
The word of his grace shall comfort us
    through :
Not fearing or doubting, with Christ on our
    side,
We hope to die shouting,—The Lord will
    provide.

79   **L. M.**
            For sustaining grace.

MY hope, my all, my Saviour thou ;
    To thee, lo, now my soul I bow ;
I feel the bliss thy wounds impart,—
I find thee, Saviour, in my heart.

2 Be thou my strength,—be thou my way ;
Protect me through my life's short day :
In all my acts may wisdom guide,
And keep me, Saviour, near thy side.

3 In fierce temptation's darkest hour,
Save me from sin and Satan's power ;
Tear every idol from thy throne,
And reign, my Saviour, reign alone.

4 My suff'ring time shall soon be o'er ;
Then shall I sigh and weep no more :
My ransom'd soul shall soar away,
To sing thy praise in endless day.

80   **4 lines 7s.**
            The pilgrim's song.

CHILDREN of the heavenly King,
    As we journey let us sing ;
Sing our Saviour's worthy praise,
Glorious in his works and ways.

2 We are trav'ling home to God,
In the way our fathers trod;
They are happy now, and we
Soon their happiness shall see.

3 O ye banish'd seed, be glad;
Christ our Advocate is made:
Us to save our flesh assumes,—
Brother to our souls becomes.

4 Fear not, brethren, joyful stand
On the borders of our land;
Jesus Christ, our Father's Son,
Bids us undismay'd go on.

5 Lord, obediently we'll go,
Gladly leaving all below:
Only thou our leader be,
And we still will follow thee.

CHORUS.

Let us walk in the light,
Walk in the light,
Let us walk in the light,
In the light of God.

81 . S. M.

Glory begun below.

COME, ye that love the Lord,
And let your joys be known;
Join in a song with sweet accord
While ye surround his throne.
Let those refuse to sing
Who never knew our God,
But servants of the heavenly King
May speak their joys abroad.

2 There we shall see his face,
  And never, never sin;
There, from the rivers of his grace,
  Drink endless pleasures in:
Yea, and before we rise
  To that immortal state,
The thoughts of such amazing bliss
  Should constant joys create.

3 The men of grace have found
  Glory begun below;
Celestial fruit on earthly ground
  From faith and hope may grow:
Then let our songs abound,
  And every tear be dry:
We're marching through Immanuel's
      ground
  To fairer worlds on high.

82   10 11, 10 11.
      Journey heavenward.

() TELL me no more of this world's vain
      store,
The time for such trifles with me now is
      o'er;
A country I've found where true joys
      abound,
To dwell I'm determined on that happy
      ground.

2 The souls that believe in Paradise live,
And me in that number will Jesus receive:
My soul, don't delay—he calls thee away,
Rise, follow thy Saviour, and bless the glad
      day.

3 No mortal doth know what he can bestow,
What light, strength, and comfort—go after
 him, go;
' Lo, onward I move to a city above,
None guesses how wondrous my journey
 will prove.

4 Great spoils I shall win from death, hell,
 and sin,
'Midst outward afflictions shall feel Christ
 within:
And when I'm to die, receive me, I'll cry,
For Jesus hath loved me, I cannot tell why.

5 But this I do find, we two are so join'd,
He'll not live in glory and leave me behind:
So this is the race I'm running through
 grace,
Henceforth—till admitted to see my Lord's
 face.

83   C. M.
Triumphant joy.

MY God, the spring of all my joys,
 The life of my delights,
The glory of my brightest days,
 And comfort of my nights:—

2 In darkest shades, if thou appear,
 My dawning is begun;
Thou art my soul's bright morning star,
 And thou my rising sun.

3 The opening heavens around me shine
 With beams of sacred bliss,
If Jesus shows his mercy mine,
 And whispers I am his.

4 My soul would leave this heavy clay
  At that transporting word,
Run up with joy the shining way,
  To see and praise my Lord.

5 Fearless of hell and ghastly death,
  I'd break through every foe;
The wings of love and arms of faith
  Would bear me conqu'ror through.

84

Rock higher than I.

IN seasons of grief to my God I'll repair,
  When my heart is o'erwhelm'd with sor-
    row and care,
From the ends of the earth unto thee will
    I cry,
Lead me to the Rock that is higher than I,
  Higher than I, higher than I,
Lead me to the Rock that is higher than I.

2 When Satan, the tempter, comes in like
    a flood,
To drive my poor soul from the fountain of
    good,
I'll pray to the Lord who for sinners did
    die,—
Lead me to the Rock that is higher than I,
  Higher than I, higher than I, etc.

3 And when I have finish'd my pilgrimage
    here,
Complete in Christ's righteousness I shall
    appear,
In the swellings of Jordan all dangers defy,
And look to the Rock that is higher than I,
  Higher than I, higher than I, etc.

4 And when the last trumpet shall sound
     through the skies,
And the dead from the dust of the earth
     shall arise,
Transported I'll join with the ransom'd on
     high
To praise the great Rock that is higher
     than I !
    Higher than I, higher than I, etc.

85

Soldiers of the Cross.

YE soldiers of the cross, rise, and put your
     armor on ;
March to the city of the new Jerusalem ;
Jesus gives the order, and leads his people
     on
'Till victory is won.
    Glory, glory, halleluiah !
    Glory, glory, halleluiah !
    Glory, glory, halleluiah !
     We are marching on.

2 The watchmen they are crying, attend the
     trumpet's sound,
Take the gospel banner, the powers of hell
     surround,
Your arms and hearts make ready, the bat-
     tle is at hand;
Go forth at Christ's command.
    Glory, glory, halleluiah !
    Glory, glory, halleluiah !
    Glory, glory, halleluiah !
     We are marching on.

3 Lay hold upon the Saviour by faith's vic-
    torious shield,
March on in order 'till you win the glorious
    field ;
Faint not by the way, till you've gained that
    peaceful shore
Where war shall be no more.
    Glory, glory, halleluiah !
    Glory, glory, halleluiah !
    Glory, glory, halleluiah !
    We are marching on.

4 Ne'er think the victory won, nor lay your
    armor down,
March on in duty, 'till you gain the starry
    crown ;
And when the war is o'er, and the battle
    you have won,
Jesus will say, " well done."
    Glory, glory, halleluiah !
    Glory, glory, halleluiah !
    Glory, glory, halleluiah !
    We are marching on.

86   8 lines 8s.
All-sufficiency of Jesus.

HOW tedious and tasteless the hours
    When Jesus no longer I see !
Sweet prospects, sweet birds, and sweet
    flowers
    Have all lost their sweetness to me ;—
The midsummer's sun shines but dim,
    The fields strive in vain to look gay ;
But when I am happy in Him,
    December's as pleasant as May.

2 His name yields the richest perfume,
  And sweeter than music his voice;
His presence disperses my gloom,
  And makes all within me rejoice:
I should, were he always thus nigh,
  Have nothing to wish or to fear;
No mortal so happy as I,—
  My summer would last all the year.

3 Content with beholding his face,
  My all to his pleasure resign'd,
No changes of season or place
  Would make any change in my mind:
While blest with a sense of his love,
  A palace a toy would appear;
And prisons would palaces prove
  If Jesus would dwell with me there.

4 My Lord, if indeed I am thine,
  If thou art my sun and my song,
Say, why do I languish and pine?
  And why are my winters so long?
O drive these dark clouds from my sky;
  Thy soul-cheering presence restore;
Or take me to thee up on high,
  Where winter and clouds are no more.

87

O how He loves!

THERE'S a Friend above all others,
    O how he loves!
His is love beyond a brother's,
    O how he loves!
Earthly friends may fail and leave us,
This day kind, to-morrow grieve us,
But this friend will ne'er deceive us.
    O how he loves!

2 Blessed Jesus, wouldst thou know him?
  O how he loves!
Give thyself e'en this day to him,
  O how he loves!
Is it sin that pains and grieves thee,
Unbelief and trials tease thee,
Jesus can from all release thee,
  O how he loves!

3 All thy sins shall be forgiven,
  O how he loves!
Backward all thy foes be driven,
  O how he loves!
Best of blessings he'll provide thee,
Naught but good shall e'er betide thee,
Safe to glory he will guide thee;
  O how he loves!

88   886, 886.

Gratitude evinced by living to God's glory.

BE it my only wisdom here
  To serve the Lord with filial fear,
   With loving gratitude:
Superior sense may I display,
By shunning every evil way,
   And walking in the good.

2 O may I still from sin depart;
A wise and understanding heart,
   Jesus, to me be given;
And let me through thy Spirit know
To glorify my God below,
   And find my way to heaven.

89

87, 87, 87, 87.

Taking up the Cross.

JESUS, I my cross have taken,
  All to leave and follow thee:
Naked, poor, despised, forsaken,
  Thou, from hence, my all shalt be.
Perish, every fond ambition—
  All I've sought, or hoped, or known:
Yet how rich is my condition—
  God and heaven are still my own!

2 Haste thee on from grace to glory,
  Arm'd by faith, and wing'd by prayer;
Heaven's eternal days before thee,
  God's own hand shall guide thee there.
Soon shall close thine earthly mission,
  Soon shall pass thy pilgrim days:
Hope shall change to glad fruition—
  Faith to sight, and prayer to praise.

90

87, 87, 47.

The pilgrim's guide and guardian.

GUIDE me, O thou great Jehovah,
  Pilgrim through this barren land:
I am weak, but thou art mighty;
  Hold me with thy powerful hand;
    Bread of heaven,
  Feed me till I want no more.

2 When I tread the verge of Jordan,
  Bid my anxious fears subside:
Bear me through the swelling current;
  Land me safe on Canaan's side:
    Songs of praises
  I will ever give to thee.

91 L. M.

Dying, rising, reigning.

HE dies! the Friend of sinners dies!
Lo! Salem's daughters weep around;
A solemn darkness vails the skies,
A sudden trembling shakes the ground:
Come, saints, and drop a tear or two
For him who groan'd beneath your load;
He shed a thousand drops for you,—
A thousand drops of richer blood.

2 Here's love and grief beyond degree:
The Lord of glory dies for man!
But lo! what sudden joys we see!   .
Jesus, the dead, revives again.
The rising God forsakes the tomb;
(In vain the tomb forbids his rise:)
Cherubic legions guard him home,
And shout him welcome to the skies.

3 Break off your tears, ye saints, and tell
How high your great Deliv'rer reigns;
Sing how he spoil'd the hosts of hell,
And led the monster death in chains:
Say, Live forever, wondrous King!
Born to redeem, and strong to save;
Then ask the monster, Where's thy sting?
And, Where's thy victory, boasting grave?

92 L. M.

Ashamed of Jesus.

JESUS, and shall it ever be,
A mortal man ashamed of thee!
Ashamed of thee, whom angels praise,—
Whose glories shine through endless days!

2 Ashamed of Jesus!—that dear Friend
On whom my hopes of heaven depend!
No!—when I blush, be this my shame—
That I no more revere his Name.

3 Ashamed of Jesus!—yes, I may,
When I've no guilt to wash away;
No tear to wipe, no good to crave,
No fears to quell, no soul to save.

4 Till then—nor is my boasting vain—
Till then, I boast a Saviour slain;
And O, may this my glory be—
That Christ is not ashamed of me.

93

Excellence of Christ.

O COULD I speak the matchless worth,
  O could I sound the glories forth,
   Which in my Saviour shine;
I'd soar and touch the heavenly strings,
And vie with Gabriel while he sings
   In notes almost divine.

2 I'd sing the precious blood he spilt,
My ransom from the dreadful guilt
   Of sin and wrath divine;
I'd sing his glorious righteousness,
In which all-perfect, heavenly dress
   My soul shall ever shine.

3 Soon the delightful morn will come
When my dear Lord will bring me home,
   And I shall see his face:
Then with my Saviour, Brother, Friend,
A bless'd eternity I'll spend,
   Triumphant in his grace.

94   86, 86, 88, 86.
All is well.

WHAT'S this that steals upon my frame?
   Is it death? is it death?
That soon shall quench this vital flame?
   Is it death? is it death?
If this be death, I soon shall be
From every pain and sorrow free;
I shall the King of glory see:
   All is well, all is well.

2 Weep not, my friends, weep not for me;
   All is well, all is well:
My sins are pardon'd—I am free;
   All is well, all is well.
There's not a cloud that doth arise,
To hide my Saviour from my eyes:
I soon shall mount the upper skies:
   All is well, all is well.

3 Tune, tune your harps, ye saints in glory;
   All is well, all is well:
I will rehearse the pleasing story;
   All is well, all is well.
Bright angels are from glory come;
They're round my bed, they're in my room;
They wait to waft my spirit home:
   All is well, all is well.

4 Hark, hark! my Lord and Master calls me;
   All is well, all is well:
I soon shall see his face in glory;
   All is well, all is well.
Farewell, my friends, adieu, adieu,
I can no longer stay with you,
My glittering crown appears in view:
   All is well, all is well.

5 Hail, hail, all hail! ye blood-wash'd throng,
    Saved by grace, saved by grace;
I come to join your rapturous song,
    Saved by grace, saved by grace:
All is peace and joy divine,
And heaven and glory now are mine;
O halleluiah to the Lamb!
    All is well, all is well.

———◆———

HEAVEN.

95   **C. M.**

The promised land.

ON Jordan's stormy banks I stand,
    And cast a wishful eye
To Canaan's fair and happy land,
    Where my possessions lie.

2 No chilling winds, or pois'nous breath
    Can reach that healthful shore;
Sickness and sorrow, pain and death,
    Are felt and fear'd no more.

3 When shall I reach that happy place,
    And be forever blest?
When shall I see my Father's face,
    And in his bosom rest?

4 Fill'd with delight, my raptured soul
    Would here no longer stay:
Though Jordan's waves around me roll,
    Fearless I'd launch away.

96　　　　　C. M.
Heavenly rest in anticipation.

WHEN I can read my title clear
　To mansions in the skies,
I'll bid farewell to every fear,
　And wipe my weeping eyes.

2 Should earth against my soul engage,
　And fiery darts be hurl'd,
Then I can smile at Satan's rage,
　And face a frowning world.

3 Let cares like a wild deluge come,
　Let storms of sorrow fall,—
So I but safely reach my home,
　My God, my heaven, my all.　　　．

4 There I shall bathe my weary soul
　In seas of heavenly rest,
And not a wave of trouble roll
　Across my peaceful breast.

CHORUS.

And you'll sing halleluiah,
And I'll sing halleluiah,
And we'll all sing halleluiah,
　When we arrive at home.

97　　　　　886, 886.
Bliss-inspiring hope.

COME on, my partners in distress,
　My comrades through the wilderness,
　Who still your bodies feel:
Awhile forget your griefs and fears,
And look beyond this vale of tears,
　To that celestial hill.

2 Beyond the bounds of time and space,
Look forward to that heavenly place,
  The saints' secure abode;
On faith's strong eagle pinions rise,
And force your passage to the skies,
  And scale the mount of God.

3 Who suffer with our Master here,
We shall before his face appear,
  And by his side sit down:
To patient faith the prize is sure;
And all that to the end endure
  The cross, shall wear the crown.

4 Thrice blessed, bliss-inspiring hope!
It lifts the fainting spirits up;
  It brings to life the dead:
Our conflicts here shall soon be past,
And you and I ascend at last,
  Triumphant with our Head.

98   4 lines 11s.
I would not live alway.

I WOULD not live alway; I ask not to stay
  Where storm after storm rises dark o'er
    the way;   ·
The few lurid mornings that dawn on us
    here
Are enough for life's joys, full enough for
    its cheer.

2 I would not live alway; no—welcome the
    tomb!
Since Jesus hath lain there, I dread not its
    gloom:
There sweet be my rest till he bid me arise,
To hail him in triumph descending the
    skies.

3 Who, who would live alway, away from
    his God—
Away from yon heaven, that blissful abode,
Where rivers of pleasure flow bright o'er the
    plains,
And the noontide of glory eternally reigns?

4 There saints of all ages in harmony meet,
Their Saviour and brethren transported to
    greet;
While anthems of rapture unceasingly roll,
And the smile of the Lord is the feast of
    the soul.

99   8s & 7s.
Heaven discerned.

MY days are gliding swiftly by,
    And I, a pilgrim stranger,
Would not detain them as they fly—
    Those hours of toil and danger.

2 We'll gird our loins, my brethren dear,
    Our heavenly home discerning;
Our absent Lord has left us word,
    Let every lamp be burning.

3 Let sorrow's rudest tempest blow,
    Each cord on earth to sever;
Our King says, "Come," and there's our
    home,
    Forever, O! forever.

CHORUS.
For O! we stand on Jordan's strand,
    Our friends are passing over;
And, just before, the shining shore
    We may almost discover.

100

The full assurance of hope.

HOW happy every child of grace,
  Who knows his sins forgiven!
This earth, he cries, is not my place;
  I seek my place in heaven:
A country far from mortal sight,
  Yet O! by faith I see
The land of rest, the saints' delight,—
  The heaven prepared for me.

2 O what a blessed hope is ours!
  While here on earth we stay,
We more than taste the heavenly powers,
  And antedate that day:
We feel the resurrection near,—
  Our life in Christ conceal'd,—
And with his glorious presence here
  Our earthen vessels fill'd.

CHORUS.

O heaven! sweet heaven!
  Heaven of the blest!
How I long to be there, in its glories
    to share,
  And to lean on Jesus's breast.

101

Beautiful Zion.

BEAUTIFUL Zion, built above,
  Beautiful city, that I love,
Beautiful gates of pearly white,
Beautiful temple,—God its light!
He who was slain on Calvary
Opens those pearly gates to me.

2 Beautiful crowns on every brow,
Beautiful palms the conqu'rors show,
Beautiful robes the ransom'd wear,
Beautiful all who enter there!
Thither I press with eager feet;
There shall my rest be long and sweet.

3 Beautiful throne for Christ our King,
Beautiful songs the angels sing,
Beautiful rest, all wanderings cease,
Beautiful home of perfect peace!
There shall my eyes the Saviour see;
Haste to this heavenly home with me.

102   10s & 4s.
Homeward bound.

OUT on an ocean all boundless we ride,
    We're homeward bound;
Toss'd on the waves of a rough, restless
        tide,
    We're homeward bound;
Far from the safe, quiet harbor we've rode,
Seeking our Father's celestial abode,
Promise of which on us each he bestow'd,
    We're homeward bound.

2 Wildly the storm sweeps us on as it roars,
    We're homeward bound;
Look! yonder lie the bright heavenly shores,
    We're homeward bound;
Steady, O pilot! stand firm at the wheel;
Steady! we soon shall outweather the gale:
O how we fly 'neath the loud-creaking sail!
    We're homeward bound.

3 We'll tell the world, as we journey along,
   We're homeward bound;
Try to persuade them to enter our throng,
   We're homeward bound;
Come, trembling sinner, forlorn and op-
     press'd,
Join in our number, O come and be blest!
Journey with us to the mansions of rest,
   We're homeward bound.

4 Into the harbor of heaven now we glide,
   We're home at last;
Softly we drift on its bright silver tide,
   We're home at last;
Glory to God! all our dangers are o'er,
We stand secure on the glorified shore.
Glory to God! we will shout evermore,
   We're home at last.

103   L. M.
Going home.

MY heavenly home is bright and fair;
  Nor pain nor death can enter there;
Its glittering towers the sun outshine:
That heavenly mansion shall be mine.

CHORUS.

I'm going home, I'm going home,
I'm going home to die no more;
To die no more, to die no more,
I'm going home to die no more.

2 My Father's house is built on high,
Far, far above the starry sky:
When from this earthly prison free,
That heavenly mansion mine shall be.

3 Let others seek a home below,
Which flames devour, or waves o'erflow;
Be mine the happier lot to own
A heavenly mansion near the throne.

4 Then fail this earth, let stars decline,
And sun and moon refuse to shine,
All nature sink and cease to be,
That heavenly mansion stands for me.

104   8 lines 10s.

Triumph.

JOYFULLY, joyfully onward I move,
  Bound for the land of bright spirits
      above;
Angelic choristers sing as I come,
"Joyfully, joyfully haste to thy home."
Soon, with my pilgrimage ended below,
Home to that land of delight will I go;
Pilgrim and stranger no more shall I roam,
Joyfully, joyfully resting at home.

2 Friends fondly cherish'd have pass'd on
      before;
Waiting, they watch me approaching the
      shore;
Singing, to cheer me through death's chill-
      ing gloom,
"Joyfully, joyfully haste to thy home."
Sounds of sweet melody fall on my ear;
Harps of the blessed, your voices I hear!
Rings with the harmony heaven's high
      dome,
"Joyfully, joyfully haste to thy home."

3 Death, with thy weapons of war lay me
    low ;
Strike, king of terrors, I fear not thy blow ;
Jesus hath broken the bars of the tomb :
Joyfully, joyfully will I go home.
Bright will the morn of eternity dawn ;
Death shall be banish'd, his scepter be gone :
Joyfully then shall I witness his doom ;
Joyfully, joyfully, safely at home.

105
Rest for the weary.

IN the Christian's home in glory,
    There remains a land of rest ;
There my Saviour's gone before me,
    To fulfill my soul's request.

CHORUS.

There is rest for the weary,
There is rest for the weary,
There is rest for the weary,
    There is rest for you.
On the other side of Jordan,
In the sweet fields of Eden,
Where the tree of life is blooming,
    There is rest for you.

2 He is fitting up my mansion,
    Which eternally shall stand,
For my stay shall not be transient
    In that holy, happy land.

3 Sing, O ! sing, ye heirs of glory ;
    Shout your triumphs as you go ;
Zion's gates will open for you,
    You will find an entrance through.

106
No sorrow there.
S. M.

O! sing to me of heaven
  When I am called to die!
Sing songs of holy ecstasy,
  To waft my soul on high.

CHORUS.

There'll be no sorrow there,
There'll be no sorrow there.
In heaven above, where all is love,
There'll be no sorrow there.

2 When cold and sluggish drops
  Roll off my marble brow,
Break forth in songs of joyfulness,
  Let heaven begin below.

3 When the last moments come,
  O watch my dying face,
To catch the bright seraphic gleam
  Which o'er my features plays.

4 Then to my raptured ear
  Let one sweet song be given;
Let music charm me last on earth,
  And greet me first in heaven.

5 Then close my sightless eyes,
  And lay me down to rest;
And fold my pale and icy hands
  Upon my lifeless breast.

6 Then round my senseless clay
  Assemble those I love;
And sing of heaven, delightful heaven,
  My glorious home above.

107

Heaven is my home.

I'M but a stranger here,
    Heaven is my home.
Earth is a desert drear,
    Heaven is my home.
    Dangers and sorrows stand
    Round me on every hand,
    Heaven is my Father-land,
    Heaven is my home.

2 What though the tempests rage,
    Heaven is my home.
Short is my pilgrimage,
    Heaven is my home.
    Time's cold and wintry blast
    Soon will be overpast,
    I shall reach home at last,
    Heaven is my home.

3 There at my Saviour's side,
    Heaven is my home.
I shall be glorified,
    Heaven is my home.
    There are the good and blest,
    Those I love most and best;
    There, too, I soon shall rest,
    Heaven is my home.

108
10s & 4s.
The pilgrim's rest.

HERE o'er the earth as a stranger I roam,
    Here is no rest, here is no rest!
Here as a pilgrim I wander alone,
    Yet I am blest, yet I am blest!

For I look forward to that glorious day
When sin and sorrow shall vanish away;
My heart doth leap while I hear Jesus say
  There, there is rest, there is rest!
2 Here are afflictions and trials severe,
  Here is no rest, here is no rest!
Here I must part with the friends I hold
    dear,
  Yet I am blest, yet I am blest!
Sweet is the promise I read in his word:
Blessed are those who have died in the Lord,
They have been called to receive their re-
    ward.
  There, there is rest, there is rest!

109

World of light.

THERE is a beautiful world
  Where saints and angels sing,
A world where peace and pleasure reigns,
  And heavenly praises ring.

CHORUS.

We'll be there, we'll be there;
  Palms of vict'ry, crowns of glory,
We shall wear
  In that beautiful world on high.

2 There is a beautiful world,
  Unseen to mortal sight;
And darkness never enters there:
  That home is fair and bright.

3 There is a beautiful world
  Of harmony and love;
O may we safely enter there,
  And dwell with God above.

110
At home in heaven.

S. M.

FOREVER with the Lord!
  Amen, so let it be!
Life from the dead is in that word,
  'Tis immortality.

2 Here in the body pent,
  Absent from Him I roam ;
Yet nightly pitch my moving tent
  A day's march nearer home.

3 Forever with the Lord
  Father, if 'tis thy will,
The promise of that faithful word,
  E'en here to me fulfill.

4 So, when my latest breath
  Shall rend the vail in twain,
By death I shall escape from death,
  And life eternal gain.

5 Knowing as I am known,
  How shall I love that word,
And oft repeat before the throne,
  Forever with the Lord !

111
Encouragement.

O WHEN shall I see Jesus,
  And dwell with him above?
To drink the flowing fountains
  Of everlasting love?
When shall I be deliver'd
  From this vain world of sin,
And with my blessed Jesus,
  Drink endless pleasures in?

2 Through grace I am determin'd
  To conquer though I die,
And then away to Jesus
  On wings of love I'll fly;
Farewell to sin and sorrow,
  I bid you all adieu;
And you, my friends, prove faithful
  And on your way pursue.

3 And if you meet with trials,
  And troubles on your way,
Cast all your care on Jesus,
  And don't forget to pray;
Gird on the heavenly armor
  Of faith, and hope, and love,
And when your race is ended,
  You'll reign with him above.

4 O do not be discouraged,
  For Jesus is your friend,
And if you lack for knowledge,
  He'll not refuse to lend;
Neither will he upbraid you,
  Though ofttimes you request;
He'll give you grace to conquer,
  And take you home to rest.

112   8s.
What must it be to be there!

WE speak of the realms of the bless'd,
  That country so bright and so fair,
And oft are its glories confess'd;
  But what must it be to be there!

2 We speak of its pathways of gold,
   Its walls deck'd with jewels so rare,
Its wonders and pleasures untold;
   But what must it be to be there!

3 We speak of its freedom from sin,
   From sorrow, temptation, and care.
From trials without and within;
   But what must it be to be there!

4 We speak of its service of love,
   The robes which the glorified wear,
The church of the first-born above;
   But what must it be to be there!

5 Do thou, Lord, 'mid sorrow and woe,
   Still for heaven my spirit prepare,
And shortly I also shall know,
   And feel, what it is to be there!

113   886, 886.

The pilgrim's happy lot.

HOW happy is the pilgrim's lot;
  How free from every anxious thought,
   From worldly hope and fear!
Confined to neither court nor cell,
His soul disdains on earth to dwell,
   He only sojourns here.

2 This happiness in part is mine,
Already saved from low design,
   From every creature love;
Blest with the scorn of finite good,
My soul is lighten'd of its load,
   And seeks the things above.

3 There is my house and portion fair;
My treasure and my heart are there,
    And my abiding home;
For me my elder brethren stay,
And angels beckon me away,
    And Jesus bids me come.

4 I come, thy servant, Lord, replies;
I come to meet thee in the skies,
    And claim my heavenly rest!
Soon will the pilgrim's journey end;
Then, O my Saviour, Brother, Friend,
    Receive me to thy breast!

114

Sweet home.

'MID scenes of confusion and creature
        complaints,
How sweet to my soul is communion with
        saints;
To find at the banquet of mercy there's
        room,
And feel in the presence of Jesus at home.

CHORUS.

Home, home, sweet, sweet home,
    Prepare me, dear Saviour, for glory, my
        home.

2 While here in the valley of conflict I stay,
O give me submission and strength as my
        day;
In all my afflictions to thee would I come,
Rejoicing in hope of my glorious home.

3 The days of my exile are passing away,
The time is approaching when Jesus will
    say,
Well done, faithful servant, sit down on my
    throne,
And dwell in my presence forever at home.

Home, home, sweet, sweet home,
O there I shall rest with my Saviour at
    home.

115

Sorrow shall come again no more.

WHAT to me are earth's pleasures, and
    what its flowing tears?
What are all the sorrows I deplore?
There's a song ever swelling still lingers
    on my ears:
O, sorrow shall come again no more!

CHORUS.

'Tis a song from the home of the weary;
Sorrow, sorrow is forever o'er;
Happy now—ever happy on Canaan's
    peaceful shore,
O, sorrow shall come again no more!

2 'Tis a note that is wafted across the troub-
    led wave;
'Tis a song that I've heard upon the shore;
'Tis a sweet-thrilling murmur around the
    Christian's grave:
O, sorrow shall come again no more!

3 'Tis the loud pealing anthem—the victor's
        holy song,
Where the strife and the conflict are o'er;
When the saved ones forever in joyous
        notes prolong,
O, sorrow shall come again no more!

116   C. M.
The prospect joyous.

AND let this feeble body fail,
   And let it faint or die;
My soul shall quit the mournful vale,
   And soar to worlds on high:
Shall join the disembodied saints,
· And find its long-sought rest,—
That only bliss for which it pants,·
   In the Redeemer's breast.

2 In hope of that immortal crown
   I now the cross sustain,
And gladly wander up and down,
   And smile at toil and pain:
I suffer on my threescore years,
   Till my Deliv'rer come,
And wipe away his servant's tears,
   And take his exile home.

3 O what are all my suff'rings here,
   If, Lord, thou count me meet
With that enraptured host to' appear,
   And worship at thy feet!
Give joy or grief, give ease or pain,
   Take life or friends away,
But let me find them all again
   In that eternal day.

117
The crown for me.

THE road that many travel
    Is not the road for me;
It leads to death and sorrow,
    In it I would not be.
But there's a road that leads to God,
It's marked by Christ's most precious blood,
    The passage here is free.
        O that's the road for me, etc.

2 The pearl that worldlings covet
    Is not the pearl for me;
Its beauty fades as quickly
    As sunshine on the sea.
But there's a pearl sought by the wise,
It's called the pearl of greatest price,
    Though few its value see.
        O that's the pearl for me, etc.

3 The hope that sinners cherish
    Is not the hope for me;
Most surely will they perish,
    Unless from sin made free.
But there's a hope that's fixed in God,
It leads the soul to keep his word,
    And sinful pleasures flee.
        O that's the hope for me, etc.

4 The crown that decks the monarch
    Is not the crown for me—
It dazzles but a moment;
    Its brightness soon will flee.
But there's a crown prepared above
For those who walk in humble love;
    Forever bright 'twill be.
        O that's the crown for me, etc.

118
The happy land.

THERE is a happy land,
  Far, far away—
Where saints in glory stand,
  Bright, bright as day;
O how they sweetly sing,—
Worthy is our Saviour King;
Loud let his praises ring
  For evermore.

2 Come to this happy land,
  Come, come away;
Why will ye doubting stand?
  Why still delay?
O we shall happy be,
When, from sin and sorrow free,
Lord we shall live with thee,
  Blest evermore.

3 Bright in that happy land,
  Beams every eye:
Kept by a Father's hand,
  Love cannot die.
O, then, to glory run;
Be a crown and kingdom won;
And bright above the sun,
  Reign evermore.

119   C. M.
Promised Canaan.

THERE is a land of pure delight,
  Where saints immortal reign;
Infinite day excludes the night,
  And pleasures banish pain.

I want to go, I want to go, I want to
  go there too;
I want to go where Jesus is, I want to
  go there too.

2 Sweet fields beyond the swelling flood
  Stand dress'd in living green;
So to the Jews old Canaan stood,
While Jordan roll'd between.

3 Could we but climb where Moses stood,
  And view the landscape o'er,
Not Jordan's stream, nor death's cold flood,
  Should fright us from the shore.

120
Home beyond the tide.

WE are out on the ocean sailing;
  Homeward bound, we sweetly glide;
We are out on the ocean sailing
  To a home beyond the tide.

All the storms will soon be over,
Then we'll anchor in the harbor:
We are out on the ocean sailing
  To a home beyond the tide;
We are out on the ocean sailing
  To a home beyond the tide.

2 Millions now are safely landed
  Over on the golden shore;
Millions more are on their journey,
  Yet there's room for millions more.

3 You have kindred over yonder,
  On that bright and happy shore;
By and by we'll swell the number,
  When the toils of life are o'er.

4 Spread your sails, while heavenly breezes
  Gently waft our vessel on;
All on board are sweetly singing—
  Free salvation is the song.

5 When we all are safely anchor'd,
  We will shout—our trials o'er—
We will walk about the city,
  And we'll sing for evermore.

121
We shall meet again.

OUR bondage here shall end
  By and by—by and by;
From Egypt's yoke set free,
In that glorious jubilee,
And to Canaan we'll return
  By and by.

2 Though our enemies are strong,
  We'll go on—we'll go on.
If our hearts dissolve with fear,
Lo! Sinai's God is near;
While the fiery pillar moves
  We'll go on.

3 And when to Jordan's flood
  We are come—we are come,
Jehovah rules the tide,
And the waters he'll divide,
And the ransom'd hosts shall shout,
  We are come.

4 There we shall meet again
  Those we loved—those we loved ;
Our embraces shall be sweet,
At the dear Redeemer's feet,
When we meet, to part no more,
  Those we loved.

122

Shall we know each other there?

WHEN we hear the music ringing
  In the bright celestial dome,
When sweet angel voices singing
  Gladly bid us welcome home,
To the land of ancient story,
  Where the spirit knows no care,
In that land of light and glory,
  Shall we know each other there?

CHORUS.

  Shall we know each other?
  Shall we know each other?
  Shall we know each other?
  Shall we know each other there?

2 When the holy angels meet us,
  As we go to join their band ;
Shall we know the friends that greet us
  In the glorious Spirit-land?
Shall we see the same eyes shining
  On us as in days of yore?
Shall we feel their dear arms twining
  Fondly round us as before?

3 O ye weary, sad, and toss'd ones,
  Droop not, faint not, by the way !
Ye shall join the lov'd and just ones
  In the land of perfect day !

Harp strings, touch'd by angel fingers,
  Murmur'd in my raptur'd ear;
Evermore their sweet song lingers,
  "We shall know each other there."

    We shall know each other,
    We shall know each other,
    We shall know each other,
    We shall know each other there.

123
The lovely sonnet.

WHEN for the eternal world I steer,
  And seas are calm and skies are clear,
And faith in lively exercise,
And distant hills of Canaan rise,
My soul for joy then clasps her wings,
And loud her lovely sonnet sings,
        I'm going home.

2 With cheerful heart her eyes explore
Each land-mark on the distant shore,
The tree of life, the pastures green,
The pearly gates, the crystal stream;
Again for joy she clasps her wings,
And loud her lovely sonnet sings,
        I'm almost home.

3 The nearer still she draws to land,
Each moment all her powers expand;
With steady helm and free bent sail,
Her anchor drops within the vail;
With holy joy she folds her wings,
And her celestial sonnet sings,
        I'm safe at home.

124
Our eternal home.

THIS groaning earth's too dark and drear
  For the saints' eternal home,
But the city from heaven will soon be here,
We know that the moment is drawing near
  When she in her beauty will come.
Her gates of pearl we soon shall see,
  Her music we soon shall hear,
Joyous and bright will that moment be;
We'll walk in the shadow of life's fair tree,
  With our Saviour forever near.

2 We would gladly exchange a world like
      this,
  Where death triumphant reigns,
For a beautiful home in the land of bliss,
Where all is happiness, joy, and peace,
  And nothing can enter that pains.
There'll be no sorrow, no more night,
  For the darkness shall flee away;
The crucified Lamb is its glorious light,
And the saints shall walk with him in white
  In that eternal day.

3 O there the lov'd of earth shall meet,
  Whom death has sunder'd here;
Prophets and patriarchs there shall greet,
And all shall worship at Jesus' feet,
  And no separation shall fear.
Though trials and griefs await us here,
  Our conflicts will soon be o'er;
This glorious hope our hearts will cheer;
We know that the Saviour will soon appear,
  And then we shall suffer no more.

125

SHALL we sing in heaven forever—
   Shall we sing?
Shall we sing in heaven forever,
   In that happy land?
Yes! O yes! in that land, that happy land,
They that meet shall sing forever,
Far beyond the rolling river,
Meet to sing and love forever
   In that happy land!

2 Shall we know each other ever
   In that land?
Shall we know each other ever .
   In that happy land?
Yes! O yes! in that land, that happy land,
They that meet shall know each other,
Far beyond, etc.

3 Shall we sing with holy angels
   In that land?
Shall we sing with holy angels
   In that happy land?
Yes! O yes! in that land, that happy land,
Saints and angels sing forever,
Far beyond, etc.

4 Shall we rest from care and sorrow
   In that land?
Shall we rest from care and sorrow
   In that happy land?
Yes! O yes! in that land, that happy land,
They that meet shall rest forever,
Far beyond, etc.

126
Beautiful land.

A BEAUTIFUL land by faith I see,
A land of rest, from sorrow free;
The home of the ransom'd, bright and fair,
And beautiful angels, too, are there.

CHORUS.
Will you go? will you go?
Go to that beautiful land with me?
Will you go? will you go?
Go to that beautiful land?

2 That beautiful land, the City of Light,
It ne'er has known the shades of night;
The glory of God, the light of day,
Hath driven the darkness far away.

MISSIONARY.

127   L. M.
Christ's universal and everlasting kingdom.

JESUS shall reign where'er the sun
Does his successive journeys run;
His kingdom spread from shore to shore,
Till moons shall wax and wane no more.

2 From north to south the princes meet,
To pay their homage at his feet;
While western empires own their Lord,
And savage tribes attend his word.

3 To him shall endless prayer be made,
And endless praises crown his head;
His name like sweet perfume shall rise
With every morning sacrifice.

4 People and realms of every tongue
Dwell on his love with sweetest song;
And infant voices shall proclaim
Their early blessings on his name.

128
Missionary hymn.

FROM Greenland's icy mountains,
    From India's coral strand,
Where Afric's sunny fountains
    Roll down their golden sand; ·
From many an ancient river,
    From many a palmy plain,
They call us to deliver
    Their land from error's chain.

2 Shall we, whose souls are lighted
    With wisdom from on high,
Shall we to men benighted
    The lamp of life deny?
Salvation!—O salvation!
    The joyful sound proclaim,
Till earth's remotest nation
    Has learn'd Messiah's name.

3 Waft, waft, ye winds, his story,
    And you, ye waters, roll,
Till, like a sea of glory,
    It spreads from pole to pole:
Till o'er our ransom'd nature
    The Lamb for sinners slain,
Redeemer, King, Creator,
    In bliss returns to reign.

129
8 lines 7s.

The watchman's report.

WATCHMAN, tell us of the night,
  What its signs of promise are.
Trav'ler, o'er yon mountain's height,
  See the glory-beaming star.
Watchman, does its beauteous ray
  Aught of hope or joy foretell?
Trav'ler, yes, it brings the day—
  Promised day of Israel.

2 Watchman, tell us of the night;
  Higher yet that star ascends.
Trav'ler, blessedness and light,
  Peace and truth, its course portends.
Watchman, will its beams, alone,
  Gild the spot that gave them birth?
Trav'ler, ages are its own:
  See, it bursts o'er all the earth.

3 Watchman, tell us of the night,
  For the morning seems to dawn.
Trav'ler, darkness takes its flight;
  Doubt and terror are withdrawn.
Watchman, let thy wand'ring cease;
  Hie thee to thy quiet home.
Trav'ler, lo! the Prince of Peace,
  Lo! the Son of God is come.

130
Promised time is coming.

REJOICE, rejoice, the promised time is
  coming,
Rejoice, rejoice, the wilderness shall bloom;
  And Zion's children then shall sing,
The deserts all are blossoming.

Rejoice, rejoice, the promised time is com-
ing,
Rejoice, rejoice, the wilderness shall bloom.
The gospel banner, wide unfurl'd,
Shall wave in triumph o'er the world;
And every creature, bond and free,
Shall hail the glorious jubilee.

CHORUS.

Rejoice, rejoice, the promised time is
coming,
Rejoice, rejoice, the Prince of Peace
shall reign.

2 Rejoice, rejoice, the promised time is
coming,
Rejoice, rejoice, the Prince of Peace shall
reign;
And lambs shall with the leopard play,
For naught shall harm in Zion's way.
Rejoice, rejoice, the promised time is com-
ing,
Rejoice, rejoice, the Prince of Peace shall
reign;
The sword and spear, of needless worth,
Shall prune the tree and plow the earth;
And peace shall smile from shore to shore,
And nations learn to war no more.

131   7s & 6s.
The gospel banner.

NOW be the gospel banner
In every land unfurl'd;
And be the shout Hosanna
Re-echoed through the world:

Till every isle and nation,
  Till every tribe and tongue,
Receive the great salvation,
  And join the happy throng.

2 Yes, thou shalt reign forever,
  O Jesus, King of kings!
Thy light, thy love, thy favor,
  Each ransom'd captive sings:
The isles for thee are waiting,
  The deserts learn thy praise;
The hills and valleys greeting,
  The song responsive raise.

CHORUS.

Now be the gospel banner
  In every land unfurl'd;
And be the shout Hosanna
  Re-echoed through the world.

PATRIOTIC.

132   6s & 4s.

"God save the state."

GOD bless our native land:
  Firm may she ever stand,
    Through storm and night;
When the wild tempests rave,
Ruler of wind and wave,
Do thou our country save
    By thy great might.

2 For her our prayers shall rise
To God, above the skies;
   On him we wait:
Thou who art ever nigh,
Guarding with watchful eye,
To thee aloud we cry,
   God save the state.

133   664, 6664.

My country! 'tis of thee.

MY country! 'tis of thee,
  Sweet land of liberty,
   Of thee I sing:
Land where my fathers died,
Land of the pilgrim's pride,
From every mountain side
   Let freedom ring.

2 My native country! thee,
Land of the noble free,
   Thy name I love;
I love thy rocks and rills,
Thy woods and templed hills:
My heart with rapture thrills,
   Like that above.

3 Let music swell the breeze,
And ring from all the trees
   Sweet freedom's song:
Let mortal tongues awake:
Let all that breathe partake;
Let rocks their silence break—
   The sound prolong.

4 Our fathers' God! to thee,
Author of liberty!
　To thee we sing:
Long may our land be bright
With freedom's holy light;
Protect us by thy might,
　Great God, our King!

134

The Union forever.

THE banner of freedom floats proudly on
　high;
The war-cry of freemen goes up to the sky;
By the homes that we cherish, the hearts
　　that we love,
That flag shall wave proudly our children
　above.

CHORUS.

Marching along, we are marching along,
We'll gird on the armor and be march-
　　ing along.
Rebellion may dare us, to crush it we're
　　strong;
For God and our country we're march-
　　ing along.

2 The flag that our fathers died nobly to save
Shall never go down over Liberty's grave;
Still free and unfettered our eagle shall soar,
Till the reign of oppression forever is o'er.

3 From the forests of Maine, from the prai-
　　ries so grand,
One shout has arisen: God bless our fair land!
The Union forever! firm, noble, and true;
And the flag of our Union, the red, white,
　　and blue!

135

The star-spangled banner.

O! say, can you see by the dawn's early
　　light,
What so proudly we hail'd at the twi-
　　light's last gleaming?
Whose broad stripes and bright stars,
　　through the perilous fight,
　O'er the ramparts we watched, were so
　　　gallantly streaming;
And the rocket's red glare, the bombs burst-
　　ing in air,
Gave proof through the night that our flag
　　was still there.

CHORUS.

　O! say, does that star-spangled banner
　　　yet wave
　O'er the land of the free and the home
　　　of the brave?

2 O! thus be it ever, when freemen shall
　　stand
　Between their loved homes and the war's
　　　desolation!
Blessed with victory and peace, may the
　　heaven-rescued land
　Praise the Power that hath made and pre-
　　　served us a nation.
Then conquer we must, when our cause it
　　is just,
And this be our motto: "In God is our trust!"

　　And the star-spangled banner in tri-
　　　umph shall wave
　　O'er the land of the free and the home
　　　of the brave.

136
Prayer for Liberty.

ROLL on, thou joyful day,
When tyranny's proud sway,
    Stern as the grave,
Shall to the ground be hurl'd,
And freedom's flag unfurl'd,
Shall wave, throughout the world,
    O'er every slave.

2 Trump of glad jubilee,
Echo o'er land and sea
    Freedom for all:
Let the glad tidings fly,
And every tribe reply,
Glory to God on high,
    At slavery's fall.

3 Free, too, the captive mind
By darkness long confined
    In slavery's night;
The Saviour's name extend,
Virtue with freedom blend,
And full salvation send,
    With freedom's light.

PARTING.

137
S. M.
Sympathy and mutual love.

BLEST be the tie that binds
Our hearts in Christian love;
The fellowship of kindred minds
Is like to that above.

2 When we asunder part,
  It gives us inward pain;
But we shall still be joined in heart,
  And hope to meet again.

3 This glorious hope revives
  Our courage by the way;
While each in expectation lives,
  And longs to see the day.

4 From sorrow, toil, and pain,
  And sin we shall be free;
And perfect love and friendship reign
  Through all eternity.

138   87, 87, 47.
For the fullness of peace and joy.

LORD, dismiss us with thy blessing;·
  Fill our hearts with joy and peace;
Let us each, thy love possessing,
  Triumph in redeeming grace;
    O refresh us,
Traveling through this wilderness.

2 So, whene'er the signal's given
  Us from earth to call away,
Borne on angels' wings to heaven,
  Glad the summons to obey;
    May we ever
Reign with Christ in endless day.

139
Say, brothers, will you meet us?

SAY, brothers, will you meet us,
  Say, brothers, will you meet us,
Say, brothers, will you meet us
On Canaan's happy shore?

2 By the grace of God we'll meet you,
By the grace of God we'll meet you,
By the grace of God we'll meet you
Where parting is no more.

3 Jesus lives and reigns forever,
Jesus lives and reigns forever,
Jesus lives and reigns forever
On Canaan's happy shore.

4 Glory, glory, halleluiah,
Glory, glory, halleluiah,
Glory, glory, halleluiah
Forever, evermore.

140
Safety in union.

TOGETHER let us sweetly live,—
  Together let us die;
And each a starry crown receive,
  And reign above the sky.

CHORUS.

  O that will be joyful, joyful, joyful!
  O that will be joyful
  To meet to part no more;
  To meet, to part no more,
  On Canaan's happy shore,
  And sing the everlasting song
  With those who've gone before.

2 And if our fellowship below
  In Jesus be so sweet,
What height of rapture shall we know
  When round his throne we meet!

141   6s & 5s.

When shall we meet again?

WHEN shall we meet again?
　　Meet ne'er to sever?
When will peace wreathe her chain
　Round us forever?
Our hearts will ne'er repose,
Safe from each blast that blows,
In this dark vale of woes,
　Never, no, never; no, no, never.

2 Soon shall we meet again,
　Meet ne'er to sever;
Soon will peace wreathe her chain
　Round us forever.
Our hearts will then repose
Safe from all worldly woes;
Our days of praise shall close,
　Never, no, never; no, no, never.

MISCELLANEOUS.

142

THERE'S a light in the window for thee,
　　brother,
　There's a light in the window for thee;
A dear one has moved to the mansion above,
　There's a light in the window for thee.

CHORUS.

　A mansion in heaven we see,
　And a light in the window for thee;
　A mansion in heaven we see,
　And a light in the window for thee.

2 There's a crown, and a robe, and a palm,
    brother,
When from toil and from care you are free;
The Saviour has gone to prepare you a home,
    With a light in the window for thee.

3 O watch, and be faithful, and pray,
    brother,
All your journey o'er life's troubled sea;
Though afflictions assail you, and storms
    beat severe,
There's a light in the window for thee.

143

The sweetest Name.

THERE is no name so sweet on earth,
    No name so sweet in heaven,
The name, before his wondrous birth,
    To Christ, the Saviour, given.

CHORUS.

We love to sing around our King,
    And hail him blessed Jesus;
For there's no word ear ever heard
    So dear, so sweet as Jesus.

2 And when he hung upon the tree,
    They wrote this name above him,
That all might see the reason we
    For evermore must love him.

3 So now upon his Father's throne,
    Almighty to release us
From sin and pains, he gladly reigns,
    The Prince and Saviour Jesus.

144

MY latest sun is sinking fast,
My race is nearly run,
My strongest trials now are past,
My triumph is begun.

CHORUS.

O come, angel band, around me stand,
I come, behold I come;
O bear me away on your snowy wings
To my own immortal home, to my own
immortal home.

2 I know I'm nearing the holy ranks
Of friends and kindred dear;
For I brush the dews on Jordan's banks,
The crossing must be near.   .

3 I've almost gained my heavenly home,
My spirit loudly sings;
The holy ones, behold, they come!
I hear the noise of wings.

4 O bear my longing heart to Him
Who bled and died for me;
Whose blood now cleanses from all sih,
And gives me victory.

145

Marching along.

THE soldiers are gath'ring from near and
from far,
The trumpet is sounding the call for the war;
The conflict is raging, 't will be fearful and
long,
We'll gird on our armor and be marching
along.

Marching along, we are marching along,
Gird on the armor, and be marching along:
The conflict is raging, 't will be fearful and
 long,
Then gird on the armor and be marching
 along.

2 We 've enlisted for life, and will camp on
 the field,
With Christ as our Captain we never will
 yield;
The " sword of the Spirit," both trusty and
 strong,
We 'll hold in our hands as we 're marching
 along.

3 Through conflicts and trials our crowns
 we must win,
For here we contend 'gainst temptation and
 sin;
But one thing assures us, we cannot go
 . wrong,
If trusting our Saviour while marching along.

146
We 'll be gathered home.

O WHAT a cheering thought is this!
 We 'll all be gather'd home;
We soon shall dwell in endless bliss,
We 'll all be gather'd home.

We 'll wait till Jesus comes,
We 'll wait till Jesus comes,

We'll wait till Jesus comes,
Then we'll be gather'd home.

2 Our kindred dear have gone before,
  We'll all be gather'd home;
I hear them on the distant shore,
  We'll all be gather'd home.

3 When in those heavenly courts above,
  We all are gather'd home,
We'll sing the Saviour's dying love
When we are gather'd home.

147

A home in heaven.

A HOME in heaven! what a joyful thought
  As the poor man toils in his weary lot!
His heart oppressed, and with anguish
      driven,
From his home below to his home in heaven.

2 A home in heaven! as the suff'rer lies
On his bed of pain, and uplifts his eyes
To that bright home, what a joy is given,
With the blessed thought of his home in
      heaven.

3 A home in heaven! when our pleasures
      fade,
And our wealth and fame in the dust are
      laid;
And strength decays, and our health is riven,
We are happy still with our home in heaven.

4 A home in heaven! when the faint heart
      bleeds,
By the Spirit's stroke for its evil deeds;

O! then what bliss in that heart forgiven,
Does the hope inspire of a home in heaven.

5 Our home in heaven! O the glorious home,
And the Spirit, joined with the bride, says
 "Come!"
Come, seek his face, and your sins forgiven,
And rejoice in hope of your home in heaven.

148   C. M.
The world has lost its charms.

LET worldly minds the world pursue,
 It has no charms for me;
Once I admired its trifles too,
 But grace hath set me free.

CHORUS.

Going home, going home
 To dwell where Jesus is;
Going home, going home,
 Going home to die no more.

2 Its pleasures can no longer please,
 Nor happiness afford;
Far from my heart be joys like these
 Now I have seen the Lord.

3 As by the light of opening day
 The stars are all concealed,
So earthly pleasures fade away
 When Jesus is revealed.

4 Creatures no more divide my choice;
 I bid them all depart;
His name, his love, his gracious voice,
 Have fixed my roving heart.

149

Looking home.

AH! this heart is void and chill,
  'Mid earth's noisy throngings;
For my Father's mansions still
  Earnestly is longing.

CHORUS.

Looking home, looking home,
Toward the heavenly mansions
Jesus hath prepared for me
In his Father's kingdom.

2 Soon the glorious day will dawn
  Heavenly pleasures bringing;
Night will be exchanged for morn,
  Sighs give place to singing.

3 O, to be at home again,
  All for which we're sighing,
From all earthly want and pain
  To be swiftly flying.

150   4 lines 11s.

Christ in the garden.

WHILE nature was sinking in stillness to
      rest,
The last beams of daylight shone dim in the
      west;
O'er fields by the moonlight, to lonely re-
      treat,
In deep meditation I wander'd to weep.

2 While passing a garden I pausèd to hear
A voice faint and plaintive from one that
      was there;

The voice of the suff'rer affected my heart,
While pleading in anguish the poor sinner's
    part.

3 So deep were his sorrows, so fervent his
    prayers,
That down o'er his bosom roll'd sweat,
    blood, and tears:
I wept to behold him: I ask'd him his name,
He answer'd, "'T is Jesus! from heaven I
    came!

4 "I am thy Redeemer; for thee I must
    die;
The cup is most bitter, but cannot pass by;
Thy sins like a mountain are laid upon me;
And all this deep anguish I suffer for thee."

5 How sweet was that moment he bade me
    rejoice;
His smile, O how pleasant! How cheering
    his voice!
I flew from the garden to spread it abroad,
I shouted, Salvation! and Glory to God!

6 The day of bright glory is rolling around,
When, Gabriel descending, the trumpet
    shall sound;
My soul then in raptures of glory shall rise
To gaze on the Stranger with unclouded
    eyes.

151   L. M.
Star of Bethlehem.

WHEN marshaled on the nightly plain,
    The glitt'ring host bestud the sky,
One star alone, of all the train,
    Can fix the sinner's wand'ring eye.

Hark! hark! to God the chorus breaks,
  From every host, from every gem;
But one alone the Saviour speaks,
  It is the Star of Bethlehem.

2 Once on the raging seas I rode,
  The storm was loud, the night was dark,
The ocean yawned, and rudely blowed
  The wind that tossed my found'ring bark;
Deep horror then my vitals froze,
  Death-struck, I ceased the tide to stem;
When suddenly a Star arose—
  It was the Star of Bethlehem.

3 It was my guide, my light, my all;
  It bade my dark forebodings cease;
And through the storm and danger's thrall,
  It led me to the port of peace.
Now safely moor'd, my perils o'er,
  I'll sing, first in night's diadem,
Forever and for evermore,
  The Star, the Star of Bethlehem.

152   L. M.
Come to Me.

WITH tearful eyes I look around,
  Life seems a dark and stormy sea;
Yet 'midst the gloom I hear a sound,
  A heavenly whisper, "Come to me."

2 It tells me of a place of rest—
  It tells me where my soul may flee;
O, to the weary, faint, oppress'd,
  How sweet the bidding, "Come to me!"

3 Come, for all else must fail and die,
  Earth is no resting place for thee;
Heavenward direct thy weeping eye:
  I am thy portion, "Come to me."

4 O voice of mercy, voice of love,
   In conflict, grief, and agony,
Support me, cheer me from above,
   And gently whisper, "Come to me!"

153
Cheer up.

CHRISTIAN, the morn breaks sweetly o'er
      thee,
And all the midnight shadows flee;
Ting'd are the distant skies with glory,
   A beacon light hangs out for thee.

CHORUS.

Arise, arise, the light breaks o'er thee,
   Thy name is graven on the throne;
Thy home is in those worlds of glory,
 . Where thy Redeemer reigns alone.

2 Toss'd on time's rude relentless surges,
   Calmly composed, and dauntless stand,
For, lo! beyond those seas emerges
   The heights that bound the promised land.

3 Cheer up! cheer up! the day breaks o'er
      thee,   .
Bright as the summer's noontide ray,
A star-gemm'd crown and realms of glory
   Invite thy happy soul away!

154   S. M.
Good Shepherd.

I WAS a wand'ring sheep,
   I did not love the fold;
I did not love my Father's voice,
   I would not be controll'd;

I was a wayward child,
  I did not love my home;
I did not love my Shepherd's voice,
  I loved afar to roam.

2 The Shepherd sought his sheep,
  The Father sought his child;
They follow'd me o'er vale and hill,
  O'er deserts, waste, and wild;
They found me nigh to death,
  Famish'd, and faint, and lone;
They bound me with the bands of love,
  They saved the wand'ring one.

3 Jesus my Shepherd is,
  'T was he that loved my soul;
'T was he that wash'd me in his blood;
  'T was he that made me whole;
No more a wand'ring sheep,
  I love to be controll'd;
I love my tender Shepherd's voice,
  I love the peaceful fold.

155   L. M.
Doxology.

PRAISE God, from whom all blessings
    flow;
Praise him, all creatures here below;
Praise him above, ye heavenly host;
Praise Father, Son, and Holy Ghost.

FAVORITE CHORUSES.

For L. M. Hymns.

THERE is a rest remains, there is a rest re-
     mains,
There is a rest remains for the people of God.

O! HE's taken my feet out of the mire and
     the clay,
And placed them on the rock of ages.

WE'LL wait till Jesus comes,
We'll wait till Jesus comes;
We'll wait till Jesus comes,
And we'll be carried home.

FOR he has been with us,
And he still is with us,
Says he will go with us to the end.

O THE bleeding Lamb! O the bleeding Lamb!
O the bleeding Lamb! He was found worthy.

THEN we'll cross the river of Jordan,
               Happy, happy;
We'll cross the river of Jordan,
               Happy in the Lord.

O CANAAN, bright Canaan, I'm bound for
     the land of Canaan;
O Canaan it is my happy home,
I'm bound for the land of Canaan.

I LOVE the Lord, for he first loved me;
And he died on the cross for sinners.

I'M happy, I'm happy, I'm on my way to
    Zion;
I'm happy, I'm happy, I'm on my journey
    home.

O COME and will you go, will you go, will
    you go,
O come and will you go where pleasure
    never dies.

For C. M. Hymns.

WEEP, weep, mourn, mourn,
    Forsake your evil way,
And to a smiling God return
    Before the judgment-day.

THIS world is not my home,
This world is not my home,
This world's a wilderness of woe.
    This world is not my home.

HOME is sweet, home is sweet,
    On Canaan's peaceful shore;
And O! 'twill fill our souls with joy
    To meet our friends once more.

WE'LL stand the storm, it won't be long,
    We'll anchor by and by.

REMEMBER me, remember me,
  O Lord, remember me;
Remember, Lord, thy dying groans,
  And then remember me.

———

    I CAN, I will, I do believe,
    I can, I will, I do believe,
    I can, I will, I do believe
      That Jesus died for me.

———

WHAT though affliction be our lot,
  Our hearts with anguish riven;
Still never let it be forgot
  There are no tears in heaven.

———◆———

For S. M. Hymns.

WE'LL be there, we'll be there;
  Palms of victory, crowns of glory,
We shall wear
  In that beautiful world on high.

———

    WE are on our journey home,
    To the new Jerusalem.

———◆———

For P. M. Hymns.

TURN to the Lord and seek salvation,
  Sound the praise of his dear name;
Glory, honor, and salvation,
  Christ the Lord is come to reign.

I AM bound for the kingdom,   ·
Will you go to glory with me?
O! halleluiah, praise ye the Lord.

———

PALMS of victory, crowns of glory,
Palms of victory you shall bear.

———

LOOKING home, looking home
To my heavenly mansion
Jesus has prepared for me   ·
In his Father's kingdom.

———

VICTORY! victory! When we've gained the
      victory,
O how happy we shall be
When we've gained the victory.

———

I LOVE Jesus, halleluiah!
I love Jesus, yes I do;
I love Jesus, he's my Saviour;
Jesus smiles and loves me too.

INDEX OF FIRST LINES.

www.ingramcontent.com/pod-product-compliance
Lightning Source LLC
Chambersburg PA
CBHW022337020726
47500CB00004B/1160